BEFORE CROWN AND KINGDOM

MELISSA WRIGHT

BEFORE CROWN AND KINGDOM

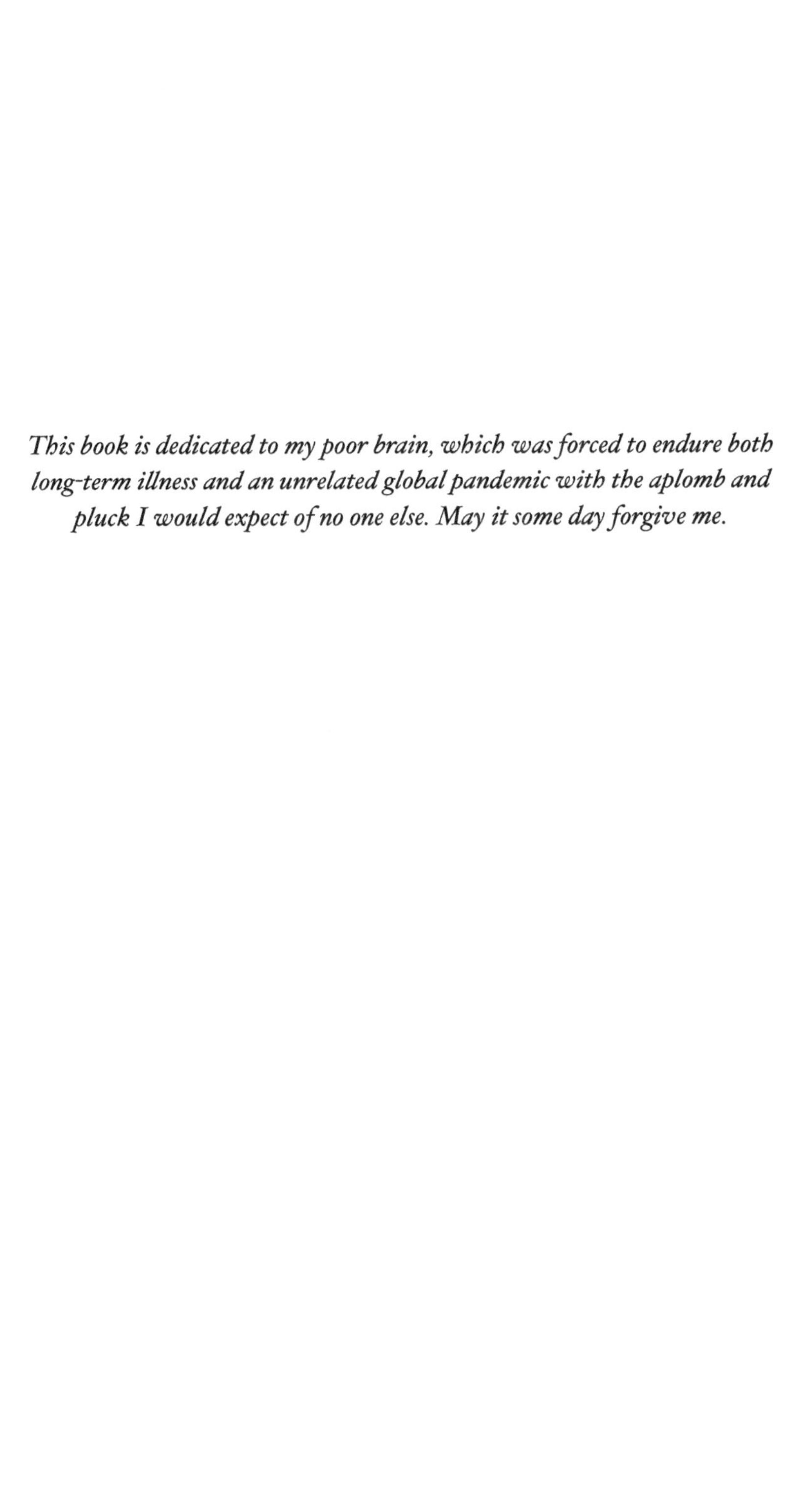

This book is dedicated to my poor brain, which was forced to endure both long-term illness and an unrelated global pandemic with the aplomb and pluck I would expect of no one else. May it some day forgive me.

CHAPTER 1

Nim had done something dangerously foolish. She stared down at the ring on her finger, unassuming as it was, a thin silver band nothing like the grandeur that surrounded her. But it was a token of vows far more significant.

The ring had been a sacrifice by Nim's mother years before. And it was the symbol of a bond that would tie her to the seneschal of Inara, head of law and order in the fight against the dark society that had nearly ruined her, a man she was so drawn to she could barely trust herself.

Fates save her, but she didn't know how she'd ended up there. For as long as she could remember, her only goal was to gain freedom. Warrick had done that for her. Warrick had broken her contract, saved her from the Trust, and helped her bind the man who'd been responsible for her torment.

And not only had she agreed to marry a seneschal, but Nim was about to be brought before his father, the king, to approve it. She felt as if she might be sick—she wasn't certain when she'd abandoned all her rules of self-preservation. Nim had gotten into perilous situations before, but she was currently feeling especially witless and wooden-headed.

"Lady Weston," a footman said from the doorway, "His Majesty will see you now."

Nim stood to follow the footman. Warrick had not been invited to attend their meeting, though she'd spent the night before wrapped in his arms. She'd been exhausted from a physical struggle that had left her bruised and battered and from plain lack of sleep. And so he'd only held her, pressing his body to hers to provide her comfort and a sense of safety she hadn't felt since she was a girl.

The man who had hurt her, Calum, was bound and imprisoned. He would never touch her again.

And Warrick had wanted her to stay. To help her. To protect her.

But morning had dawned, and with it came truths she'd managed to push aside in the rush of relief at surviving her brush with the Trust. Warrick was seneschal, and the kingdom was managed by his hand. Too soon, he'd dressed in the robes of his station, a silver coronet upon his head, and he'd left her not with the sweet murmurings of the night before but with a warning. He did not want her to speak a word of her father's bargain with the head of the Trust to the king, to reveal that Nim was bound by magic to decide the fate of the heir of Inara. "If he thinks it has any sway in my fate"—Warrick had shaken his head—"he won't allow you to remain alive."

The truth of his statement had hit her with a sensation like being doused in icy water, and the surety that came with his emotions was sharp and clear. It was not that Warrick had forgotten she could sense intimations from him, only that he'd left himself open for her to feel how very true they were. To know.

The king would see her hanged before he risked his only heir, even if that heir was only half Inaran. The head of the Trust had assured that King Stewart had been unable to produce another heir, and the alternative to Warrick as heir was unthinkable—someone who belonged wholly to the Trust.

Nim walked through a pair of massive double doors held open by two precisely dressed guards and into a chamber that felt impossibly large and empty—not of the finery that filled the entirety of the castle but of any single other soul, even the king's guards. The doors shut behind her, the finality of the sound echoing through the chamber, and Nim strode forward, a woman summoned.

King Stewart sat in a finely carved chair, a man much changed from when Nim was a girl. His blond hair had gone silvery, his face somewhat thin beneath a beard long enough for braids.

He did not seem in an entirely pleasant sort of mood, if his scowl was any indication. It was no surprise, Nim thought, after what he'd suffered. The man had likely been in nothing but foul spirits for years. Even if he was not physically tormented at the hands of the Trust like so many others, what he had endured had been its own form of torture.

Nim imagined it had been different before, when he still believed he had a chance to best the Trust. The king had openly loathed magic for as long as she could remember, but Nim had since learned that his battle with the Trust went back to before she had been born. She imagined his hatred of them had hardened to iron, if it had ever been a more malleable thing, hammered out over decades, thrust into the fire only to be plunged into the quench pit again and again.

The head of the Trust had done that. A dark and powerful queen.

Warrick's mother.

"Lady Nimona," the king said, though Nim had fallen from good society when her father was taken by the Trust.

She dipped before him anyway. She might no longer have been a lady, but she still stood before a king. "Your Majesty."

His gaze roamed over her, and Nim let herself do the same to him. As a boy, Warrick had watched the man—his father, though the secret had been kept to only his closest advisers—as he was foiled in every attempt to produce a lawful heir. A son, unlike Warrick, who was not tied to magic or the Trust. The procession of women Stewart had arranged marriages with were rumored to have gone mad from invisible torments or been stricken by unnameable disease, all while the head of the Trust had lingered in her catacombs beneath the city, laughing at him for believing he might someday succeed.

Stewart hadn't given up for the longest time, hiding the women away in towers, locking them into secret rooms. It hadn't mattered. It had never helped.

His opponent excelled at games. She had promised to make the king pay. And it was said that she had never broken a vow.

Though Stewart might have spent his waking hours devising plans to thwart her, he remained unable to call her out by name, even from the safety of his throne. He could only say that magic was at fault for what was happening in Inara and could not bring himself to stand on his dais and point to the head of the Trust as the murderer of the women who might someday carry his heirs, she who had planted a son of their own to overtake his throne. And it was good that Stewart had been cautious, because should he break the unspoken rules, there would be war. The queen would win. The kingdom would fall.

As it was, there was only one thing holding it all together—one thing that kept the two sides at an impasse, the Kingdom and the Trust only biding their time.

It was Warrick, half Inaran and half the dark magic that was the Trust.

"You favor your father." Stewart's voice was quiet but strong, his appraisal of her not entirely arguable. "Your mother was a beauty, but there"—his eye narrowed—"at the set of your mouth, I see his determination."

Nim inclined her head slightly, not mentioning that Warrick might favor the king, too, in his mannerisms and in the set of his jaw, though nothing of his coloring or the lines of his nose and brow. The king was softer, stronger, where Warrick was lethal grace, wolfish where his brother, Calum, had been more raptorial. Both had looked far more like their mother. Both had inherited her magic.

"I know nothing of where you have been the intervening years," he said, "though I know Warrick would never have let you come so near had he not already discovered every detail of your past. He keeps it from me, despite his vow that the kingdom comes first. I might not have discovered how you came into his association, but that does not mean I'm fool enough to assume it was mere coincidence."

"I've been at Hearst Manor for the last several years, Your Majesty. By the grace of the gentleman Hearst and his family—"

Her words cut off at Stewart's expression. He knew that well enough. He'd meant that he did not know what she had been up to and did not trust that she had not been compromised by magic.

Nim could not deny it. In fact, her situation was far more incriminating than merely compromised.

"I am aware that your circumstances were not of your own causing," he said, "but you should know that if not for my gratitude to your father, you would already be dead."

Nim swallowed.

His fingers, laden with heavy rings and bent as if they had not healed properly after a break, twitched against the arm of the chair.

Nim wondered how a king might have broken his hand.

"I cannot risk it. Not after everything she's done." His green eyes, not at all luminous like Warrick's, cut through her. "Your father, along with several other trusted advisers among my court, men and women who I held dear, tried to stop her." He took a slow breath. "You know how they paid. All of them."

Nim did know. Her mother had died of a mysterious illness, as had Wesley's mother and others. Nim's father had been trapped in a cell deep within the undercity, devoured by magic as a sacrifice to the Trust, payment to its queen.

"She took everything from me," Stewart said. "Everything."

Nim felt the breath catch in her chest, because the Trust had not taken Warrick. She did not know what that meant and did not understand how having Warrick so close—a reminder of all that had been stolen from him and all that was dangerous to his kingdom—might affect the king. Worse, a question waited on the tip of her tongue: whether he had taken the head of the Trust to bed willingly or been coerced by her magic. Nim bit it back. It would not matter, not when what was done was done. It was better left buried.

Stewart ran a hand over his beard, evidently distracted by his own ruminations. "She mocks me from the safety of her lair," he said, "after all these years." When his eyes met Nim's again, she did not like the resolve she saw in them. "I cannot in good conscience approve the match. Not when I cannot be certain who you are." His hand returned to its place on the chair, palm covering a carved rose that had worn dull with use. "Even if I know who you *were*."

The proper thing would have been to curtsy and leave, but Nim hadn't been proper in a long time. Besides, it was not as if she could argue his point. She was tied to magic. Her father's bargain had altered her fate. It had bound to her the king's heir. "Your Majesty, if I may, why bring me here? If you'd no intention of allowing this, why meet with me at all?" *And alone.*

His shoulders shifted, bringing him into a posture so much like the portraits she'd seen as a girl, the bearing of a king, sole leader of Inara and all who resided within its walls. "So that you understand, Lady Weston, that with one misstep from you, I will end your life"—his expression was as hard and true as any she'd ever seen—"to protect my kingdom. And my son."

CHAPTER 2

Nim stared across a lavishly decorated room, all of it trimmed in rich materials. *Her* room. In Inara Castle. She never thought she would return, and she'd certainly never believed it would be like it was. It could have been worse, she supposed. The king might have tried to tie her to a bargain. He might have traded her back to the Trust. Nim was going to have to unearth the secrets that had been kept from her and learn how the bindings of her father's bargain could be unwound. There was nothing but to discover if there was any chance to get free, to save herself from the wrath of a king, under whose roof she found herself.

Her gaze rested on a pair of steel scissors so fine they might have cost more than her entire wardrobe at Hearst Manor.

"Is there anything I can get you, my lady?"

Nim shook herself from her thoughts. Her new maid was pretty, with a round face, dark eyes, and a black dress fitted snugly over her petite frame. Her hair had been drawn back into a tight knot of braid beneath a small cap. "Thank you, Maris, but no." Nim watched her rearrange a set of finely carved wood brushes on the vanity then resituate the linens in a drawer.

"Maris," she said after a moment, "what is it that you are tasked with, precisely?"

The maid turned to face her. "Only you, my lady." Her smile was soft and sweet, and the ease of her manner was already working its charm on Nim.

"Me?"

Maris nodded, bringing her hands to clasp loosely at her waist in a gesture that painfully reminded Nim of Allister, the gentleman Hearst's valet whom Nim had stolen for her own. "Yes, my lady. Whatever you desire, it has been set upon my head to see it done. I will oversee the matter of meals and baths, source your wardrobe, and manage your maids. I am to be available at all hours for your bidding"—she gestured to a door on the far side of the room—"right through that doorway at any time, day or night. I will walk with you through the castle and accompany you, should you wish to leave the grounds. You'll have guards off the property, but here, I am to be your protection."

Nim tried to school her surprise. It did not work.

The maid's smile widened. "Lord Warrick requires that all of the lady's maids are competent in defense to at least some degree and that no lady is left unattended where she might be at risk."

Because of the others, Nim realized, *the women who had been burned at the hands of the Trust.* "Thank you," she said, her voice breathier than she liked. "I appreciate your candor, and I hope that I am not too much of a bother to you."

"It is no bother at all, my lady. You are my charge."

She said it as if the duty was an honor, and Nim wondered what the seneschal had told her, what sort of lady the maid thought she was serving. "So," Nim said slowly, "what is it that we are to do now?"

Maris's smirk implied that Nim had hit the heart of the matter. "Lord Warrick has instructed me that you are to take time to settle in because you are not to be assigned to your post until you are comfortable and ready to begin." She shrugged. "Until then, we could take a walk through the gardens, tour the stables, or anything at all that might please you. There's a ball to be planned for and a gathering of advisers soon. But you are at your leisure."

Nim pursed her lips. She'd not had much experience with leisure and wasn't certain she was going to like it. "What, exactly, did Lord Warrick say my post was, again?"

Maris's eyes crinkled at the edges. "He did not say at all, my lady. But he was very specific in what your uniform should entail."

Nim bit down her response at the remembered vow he'd made to her, the low growl of approval at the mention of her unfit-for-good-society trousers. "Yes," she managed. "Thank you."

There was a light knock at the door, and the two women exchanged a glance. "Come in," Nim said, moving to stand as Wesley, the seneschal's personal messenger, edged through the doorway in his own livery.

His smile was broad and just a little bit crooked. "Nim." He gave a swift nod toward Maris. At the maid's blink, Wes cleared his throat and bowed deeply at Nim. "My lady, I am to deliver you to the seneschal posthaste, if it please you."

"I'm grateful to see you, Wesley. And please," she glanced at Maris, "both of you may call me Nim, at least when there is no one about to take issue with our familiarity."

"Yes, my lady," they echoed.

Nim gave them each a look then ran her hands over the front of her gown. "I suppose I am ready." The words came easily, but she felt nothing of the sort.

❦

As WESLEY LED Nim down myriad corridors, each filled with milling ladies and lords dressed in finery and staff about their work, Nim glanced over her shoulder at an unsettling shape in the shadows, only to find, when she looked harder, that it was gone. She had felt certain, but no one was there. The rest in the corridor appeared to pay her not a bit of mind, yet she could not shake feeling as if all eyes were on her. "Wesley," she whispered, "how unusual is it for a new lady to be installed inside the castle?"

His gaze did not stray from the path, but she felt him shift closer in their striding. "Fairly," he admitted, "though yours has not been officially announced."

"And what do you suppose will happen when I'm installed in my post?"

The edge of his mouth shifted into a pinned-on grin. "Warrick has ensured that the details of your post will not be made entirely public, my lady."

They walked past a row of armed guards, whose breastplates were stamped with the emblems of Inara and trimmed in steel and the king's colors. Nim held her tongue at any questions that might have broken free. She did not relish the idea of drawing more attention to herself than her mere presence already had.

When they finally arrived to a small study that seemed disused, dimly lit only by the late-day sun though a row of high windows, Nim felt her chest ease. But Wesley closed the door, someone moved behind her, and she startled, reaching automatically to her thigh, where her mace and dagger no longer rested.

"My lady," came Warrick's smooth voice. "I apologize."

She made a sound in her throat that she wasn't certain even she could decipher.

Warrick smiled. "Thank you, Wesley," he said after a moment. "I'll see that she's returned in time for dinner."

Wes grinned at Nim, but at Warrick's look, he snapped his expression back into place and gave a stately bow.

When he exited the room, Warrick turned to Nim. "Walk with me?"

She inclined her head then walked beside him through a long corridor empty of any courtiers or castle staff. Warrick had likely had her brought there so that no one would see them, so the seneschal and Lady Weston together would draw no attention. And still, he did not touch her but only held his head high and his shoulders straight in the posture of a king's man.

Their steps, quiet and steady, led them to another corridor then a twisting flight of stairs. It was only when they came through a small door to an even darker corridor that Nim sensed a change in Warrick. He seemed to relax as the door closed behind them in a muffled slide of wood against frame, then Warrick's magic rose warmly through her, and a row of torches flared to life.

The hall was lit by the soft glow of the magical flames, and his hand slid against her arm as he turned to face her. He brushed a thumb over her cheek, his fingers slipping into her hair as he shifted nearer. "Stewart told me his decision. I'm sorry I was not informed immediately. I would have come to you."

Nim's eyes closed as she settled into his warmth. It was no great surprise that Stewart had not disclosed how he'd threatened Nim with death should she make even one misstep. He must have only revealed that they did not have his blessing for marriage. She wasn't sure she had the heart to tell him, not when he finally held her so near.

Warrick pressed a gentle kiss to her brow. "It is not his choice to make, my lady. It is only up to him whether it is made public."

She opened her eyes to stare up at the man who had saved her, the man whose fate was tied to hers.

"I prefer having you at my side, in my rooms," Warrick told her. "It makes protecting you easier. But I won't risk your status among court when you've only just won it back."

She frowned. "I have not won it back. I'm here, in the castle, but that means nothing. I'm not sure"—she shook her head—"I'm not certain it matters to me now."

"It might." His hand slid over her shoulder and down to her waist. "Someday."

Nim remembered when Warrick had said he would never lie

to her. *Lying is for cowards*, he'd vowed. *I have nothing to fear*. But he'd found something to fear—losing her, that he would not be able to protect her—not only her reputation but her very life. She could feel it.

At her hesitance, he said, "For now, it is your choice to make. You can stay in your rooms with vetted guards at the door and at your side when you venture out, or we can complete the ceremony and announce our intentions to those who will be aware that you are staying with me." They could save themselves the repercussions of being found out, of a seneschal, head of law and order, capering about the castle with an outcast lady with ties to magic.

"But the king—"

"Does not always like what I do. That does not mean he can stop me." His words were a vow, entirely truth.

"He can stop me," she whispered. "It would be very easy for him to deal with a girl nearly no one knows is even here."

Warrick's grip tightened. "A woman," he said, "who is the seneschal's wife."

Any response Nim might have made was drowned by the intimation that came from him, swift and strong. "Thank you," she said after a moment, "for all that you have done."

His gaze danced between her eyes, then he leaned down to press a soft, lingering kiss to her lips. "I'm sorry that this has been such an adjustment for you." His words were quiet, his mouth sliding to her hair as he drew her deeper into his embrace. "Is it too terrible?"

She sighed. "I expected it to feel smaller after so many years. Like any other place I've not been since I was a girl."

He drew back to look at her.

"It's not," she said with a half smile. "Everything seems so much larger." *And terrifyingly real.*

"And irretrievably structured?"

Her smile grew. "Dreadfully so."

He stepped back, sliding his hand into hers as he turned

them toward the long corridor. "You do not have to stand on occasion with me." Not when they were alone, anyway. There was a twinkle in his eye when he glanced at her again. "I'm quite fond of your indiscretions."

Her quiet laugh echoed through the corridor. "Remember you said that, my lord."

Warrick bit his lip as he glanced at her again, a sensation rising from him that Nim could not quite interpret. As they moved farther along the corridor, with its high ceiling arched with thick beams crisscrossing overhead to meet the smooth stone walls, the torches seemed to flare a little brighter. Warrick led her past a row of portraits then turned her to face one halfway down the row.

"I'm sorry that Stewart may have been sharp with you, but trust that he has been tormented by all that he has lost. He no longer believes he has the luxury of taking chances with her."

Her, the head of the Trust, Warrick's mother and the very reason the king refused to chance Nim.

"He loved those who were taken. He loves them still. It is only made worse that they were lost in their attempt to save him and the kingdom."

Nim stared up at the painting, her fingers curled into her palms. It was her father, tall and proud, dressed in all the finery of his station as adviser to the king. And it was her papa, handsome and strong, calloused hands wrapped casually around the hilt of a sword. She stepped forward, a hitch in her breath. "Thank you," she whispered. "I haven't—I haven't seen him in so long." The last time she had, he'd looked nothing like the painting. He'd been thin and wan, his familiar dark hair and laughing eyes lost in some intangible way, the magic having taken so much from him that he'd seemed not like himself at all.

"Would you like me to have it moved to your rooms?" Warrick's tone was measured, nothing but reassurance that neither choice was wrong.

"No." She swallowed hard. "Let him rest." At the intimation

she sensed from Warrick, she looked at him, knowing trust was the only way to move forward, the only way to know more. She could not keep her secrets from him any longer. "I always thought—I was afraid to bring him to mind. Because when I was in the undercity and I thought of him…"

He stepped closer to place a hand at the small of her back. "It doesn't work that way, Nim. It's true that the desire to see him could have drawn you, that it might have been used to bring you nearer the well of magic, but any desire you have cannot affect him. It does not hurt him to be remembered. He could only have been harmed by his own desires, by his own thoughts and actions." *And you, only by your own*, he seemed to think, but Warrick did not say it. Because Warrick's desires and actions could hurt her too. There was a surety with his words, though, that said her father was long past the point of wanting and that everything she'd known of him was gone.

That, at least, was of no surprise to her.

Warrick's brow pinched, and Nim turned toward him, away from the image of a man she could no longer hope to see again. "What is it?"

"Will you tell me how it is that you came to be able to sense what was happening to you?" He wanted to know how she could tell the magic was drawing her when so many others could not, how she could feel intimations from them and know when she was being touched by someone whose energy was tied to what waited below Inara. How she had kept herself safe.

"When my father made his bargain, something"—she paused and shook her head—"something came over me. I was home in my bed, the room dark and everyone asleep." She shivered at the memory, and he ran a hand over her arm. "It was cold, unseasonably so, and my feet were bare." Her eyes met Warrick's. He still bore a tiny mark on his brow from the scuffle with his brother. "I walked all the way to the undercity in my nightclothes, alone and unafraid. I didn't remember doing it and have no earthly idea why no one stopped me, but I'll never forget what I saw there, how the torches lit my path through the catacombs, how the magic tugged me down to her rooms."

Warrick's other hand tightened against Nim's waist, but any unease he felt at the mention of his mother was kept tied within him. He had never told her such secrets—that the head of the Trust was his mother and Calum his brother.

The woman was a queen, but her kingdom was nothing like Inara. The undercity was dark and dangerous, swimming with a current of ancient magic unfathomable in its strength. "She was there, with my father, his blood trailing over his arms, pooling onto the stone floor." Nim closed her eyes. "It was as if he had no idea I was there, but she... she looked up at me, her eyes as black as onyx. Like Calum's but darker. Deeper than anything his might ever be. She smiled at me, the queen of all that power, and I could feel it beneath us, around us, lashing me tighter as she smiled... and her..."

"Nim." Warrick's tone was sharp, snapping her from the memory to jolt back alert. His concern washed over her, close and warm. He was afraid.

"I'm sorry, I..." She shook her head. "I don't—I try not to think of her."

Warrick drew her against him, folding her into an embrace. "Don't, then. Don't think of her, Nim."

As if, returned to her home, the place it all began, such a thing felt possible at all.

CHAPTER 3

When they returned to her suite, Nim glanced around the neat and tidy space, rich with lush fabrics, dark wood, and heavily cushioned chairs. "This isn't my room."

Warrick stared down at her. "I hope you don't mind. I prefer you in this one instead. I had Maris bring your things."

"My lady's maid," she said.

He replied with a low hum, his hand stroking idly over her arm. Nim pursed her lips.

"I do think I'll like her. But would it be—" She sighed. "I suppose it's impossible to have my valet."

Warrick pinned down the beginning of a smile, his hands sliding to clasp casually behind his back. "Not, I suspect, the best tactic when trying to keep a low profile." He shifted, and she had the sense he wanted to reach out to her, to touch her again.

She was fighting the same compulsion, and she hated that she would have to give up throwing decorum to the wind. It would be particularly difficult when it came to him.

"You'll be free to visit them at the manor as you wish, provided you take along Wesley or your personal guard."

"Thank you," she said. *For trusting me. For protecting me. For setting me free.* "And I'm sorry for what I did to the other guards."

Warrick's expression fell. Evidently, he had not resolved to forgive every indiscretion. "We should agree not to talk about that."

She made a show of pressing her lips tightly together.

His eyes lingered on them for longer than was commonly considered polite. "I should go," he said.

"When will I see you?" She forced her voice to sound as practical as possible, but he couldn't have been fooled. Anyone could see she was besotted with the man.

He gave her a devastating smile before he turned. "Soon enough, should the fates allow."

Nim watched him stride from the room. She'd been averse to commitment nearly all her life. Her only friends were Allister and Margery, and she'd done her level best to keep anyone she didn't want to get hurt at arm's length. The only thing she'd shoved at harder was magic. And yet, she'd chosen Warrick, despite his magic, his connections, and a warning from the king. She'd chosen him, it was terrifying, and she still had every desire to walk right through behind him.

She was still staring at the door when Maris finally came through. "Oh, my lady. I didn't realize you were back. Would you like to sup in your room this evening or go down to dinner?"

Nim glanced around the space again, her eyes catching on a fine writing desk positioned just so that light from the window would lie across its surface come morning. Upon it was the set of steel sheers from her other room. "Here," she said absently. "If it's not too much trouble."

"Of course, my lady."

As Maris turned to give instructions to various other maids, Nim made a circuit through the room, which was much more to her tastes than the other had been. She wasn't certain that was why Warrick had moved her. Her fingers trailed over the doors of a fine wardrobe with delicate leaves carved over its trim and the pulls shaped into roses. Beside it hung still-life paintings with floral themes and vining leaves, pleasant and peaceful enough, but she still missed the little painting of the sleeping dog she'd had at Hearst. She wondered if she might be allowed to bring it then smiled at the idea of such a poorly done work on castle walls. Maybe she would commission a piece, something garish and improper, from Margery's cousin.

Several chairs were scattered in the space, with two low tables nearby and a variety of trunks near the far wall. Her fingers trailed over a new set of brushes, fine bone inlaid with jewels. Brushes were such a personal thing, and it seemed strange that Maris would have replaced them... stranger still that her room had been changed at all. She glanced over her shoulder, but the maid was still putting the others to task.

A wide fireplace was centered on the largest wall, and beyond one door, Nim found a spacious bedchamber and a private bath. She sighed, leaning against the doorway as her eyes again found the writing desk. Nim's previous life had been filled with correspondence, research made in the undertakings set to her by the Trust.

She'd no idea who she might write without that need. Margery would likely throttle her for sending a letter instead of coming in person once she heard what had transpired. Warrick had sent a message to her friend Margery and to Hearst Manor for Alice and Allister, to let them know that she was safe. They had been warned to use discretion, surely, but all had known that Nim had been involved with the Trust.

They also knew that the seneschal of Inara had been involved as well. She found herself standing before the desk, unaware that she'd crossed the space, her fingers trailing across strangely familiar parchment.

"Shall I lay out your nightclothes, my lady? I'm certain today has been taxing enough that once you're finished with dinner..."

Nim nodded absently, managing to give the maid a smile before returning to her senses. "I'm sorry. You're right. I'm afraid I'm overwrought. It is a rather big change for me."

"Of course, my lady. Dinner is on its way up, and then I'll leave you to your peace. You may call if you need me, no matter the time."

"I'm grateful," Nim told her, and she meant it. She felt incredibly alone in the big, empty room, though she was still within reach of the people she loved. She was grateful, too, that she'd not been forced to leave Inara behind. And no matter what else, no matter how her mind kept returning to him, Calum was no longer her concern. He had been locked in a dungeon deep beneath the castle, safely bound by contract, magic, and iron bars.

Never mind that the king wanted her head. Calum could not touch her.

It didn't change her fate, though. It only untied her from him, not from the bargain her father had made and their ties to the magic of the Trust.

The people of Inara had long gambled at winning a boon with bargains and magic, but no one ever truly won. It was a compulsion to many. The desperate who played went further and further into debt until they could no longer see their way out. Nim's own bargain had won her no favor because hers had not been a contract she'd made herself.

Her father had bound her within his own terms, and in the end, his trade had only made her need to be near the thing her father had feared. It had caused her to be drawn to magic and those who could wield it, the very danger he'd wanted so much to subvert. But Nim could do nothing about what had happened.

All that was left for her was to figure out how to defeat the terms and their hold on her, to understand the dangerous secrets kept by the Trust. Because until she was free of the bargain her father had made, she would never be free at all.

BY THE TIME DARKNESS FELL, Nim had sent messages to her friends, saying that she would be calling on them in the following days, picked at her dinner, changed into a clean shift, and settled into a large and excessively pillowed bed. Heavy curtains draped around her, making it too dark and too quiet. It was not long before she grew restless and rose to pace the room between the strips of moonlight that cut across her floor. The door to the room where Maris slept was closed, with no light visible through the frame. Sounds did not reach her from the corridor outside or through the windows from the courtyard below. It did not keep her from being unsettled.

So many times, she had felt magic calling to her, wanting to draw her to it in a terrifying, venomous way. It was not what she felt with Warrick. She was drawn to him in a way that was far less deniable, and although not vicious, she certainly could not say it was innocuous. It was bound to get her into trouble, even without the king's warning.

She stared at the silvery moon through the delicate trim over arched windows and could not help but think of Warrick. He was under the same moonlight, in the same castle, but she could no longer slip into his rooms. He had left a hidden passageway open to her before, and she had found any manner of reasons to use it. But that had been then.

Something ticked in her chest at the thought, a small trip in her pulse, and suddenly, her feet had resumed their pacing but had gained a purpose. Warrick had not moved her for no reason, surely. He had wanted her in an entirely different suite, one illuminated by moonlight on the same side of the castle as his own. She lit a lantern from the tinderbox with trembling hands then held it high as she trailed the exterior walls of her room, the fingertips of her free hand running over the surface of each wall. It was a large room, but only so many places could hold such a secret, and near the corner opposite the fireplace, Nim discovered a familiar sort of trim carved only similarly to the others. When she slid her finger across it, the wood swung out like a wing to reveal a split in the wall.

A hidden door. She cursed, but it was the pleasant, surprised sort, twisted by her smile, and she opened the panel to dash inside without so much as donning a robe.

CHAPTER 4

Nim's lantern threw light through the narrow corridor as her feet sped over the smooth stone. A tingle of unease skittered down her spine like a phantom sensation of fingers trailing her skin, but when she turned, she found nothing but the shadows that danced in her firelight. She cautiously returned to her task. She did not have her bearings well enough to feel certain the direction to Warrick's rooms, but the passage didn't branch off more than a few times, and she could feel the pull of his magic, soft and warm, somewhere deep inside her.

When she came to a sharp turn, the corridor met with another, far more familiar, and the unease melted away. It was the passageway she'd used to gain access to his rooms, hidden by magic that Nim could sense, giving her access while any other citizen of Inara would walk right past. From where she stood, one direction would lead her out into the dark night and the center of Inara. The other led to him.

She could not help the smile that tugged at her lips as she found the paneled door leading into his rooms. She set her lantern in the alcove beside his, her flame real and true, his a flame bought by magic, and opened the door to his study.

Warrick lounged in the wide, plush chair she'd sat in count-less times, his wolfish grin gone catlike with self-satisfaction. His desk was littered with correspondence cast in a silvery glow by the moonlight through the windows. He leaned forward. "It took you longer than I thought it would."

She stepped into the room. "I'm sorry to disappoint you."

When he only smiled in response, she added, "I'm surprised you'd trust me with a way to escape the castle, not to mention wherever the other corridors go."

His eyes were on her, unnaturally green in the moonlight as she trailed her finger over the edge of his desk, lingering across the space from him.

"You know the risk," he said. "I cannot lock you away forever."

Something uncomfortable rose in her, a reminder that the king had tried just that with the women he had known. It had not worked. The head of the Trust had come for them.

It hadn't stopped Warrick from trying to cart her out of the kingdom.

She let her gaze meet his. Nim had not admitted to the man that she knew his secrets, though she wasn't fool enough to assume she knew them all. Calum was his brother, his mother was head of the Trust, and his father was king. Warrick was heir of Inara. Nim was destined to decide his fate.

And yet, Warrick had chosen to tie his life to hers. She had chosen him despite the risks of his position in the kingdom and his relationship to the Trust. They were to be married, bound, just as soon as she agreed to act against a king's wishes.

The ring felt warm on her finger, small and thin as it was, a constant reminder of her mother, the others, and what they had all sacrificed to save the kingdom from the Trust. They had sewn all of their hopes in a bargain, all of their faith in her.

"How are you to be my husband with so many secrets between us?"

Her voice was quiet, but Warrick rose slowly, sure as he

closed the distance. He stopped before her, his words a vow. "I told you, my lady, I'm bare to you. I will not lie to you."

"But I could lie to you." She stared up at him, her fingers itching to touch his chest. "There is nothing to stop me."

A corner of his lips twitched, and he reached forward to take hold of her waist, his skin warm through the thin material of her shift. He leaned down, pressed a kiss softly to her cheek, and whispered, "There is no reason to lie to me. Nothing you might say could break my vow."

His vow to protect her. His vow to make her his partner—his equal, he'd said. No matter how much his words meant or how much she wanted it, the threats still hung over her. She had to find a way to protect herself, to protect them both. "I want to know about magic."

A *hmm* rumbled in this throat. "I suspect you do. It seems you've managed quite a bit on your own, but even though you were clever enough to bind Calum, I'd rather you know whatever you need should any further complications arise." His gaze traveled over her. His intimation said that she should really not have come to his rooms wearing nothing more than a shift if she expected him to discuss the details of her new post.

It said he was toying with the idea of sending her more specific imaginings. Heat swam through her, but his gaze caught near the neck of her shift, where the exposed skin showed the edge of a jagged scar, wrought by magic, not so unlike his own scar. It still stung and pulsed, as it always would, but she could at least be grateful that the magic threaded through it was Warrick's—not Calum's, not the queen's.

"My new post?"

"Yes." His eyes came back to hers. "I've decided your talents will be quite useful in the plight to stave off the Trust."

"My talents," she echoed.

She felt the humor from him, swelling through intimations that were becoming more familiar, easier to read. She wasn't certain whether that was due to becoming more accustomed to them or if Warrick was allowing her to sense more from him.

"We can discuss it in detail tomorrow, but I'd like you to assist in inspecting the seized correspondence and reports on movements that have been submitted by the king's guard. Your familiarity with how the Trust operates will be an asset to the king."

She ran a tooth over the edge of her lip, wondering if she should tell him she'd been put on notice. "You hope to win his approval of me."

"No, love. I hope what you've been through can help put an end to this for us all."

"Warrick," she whispered after a long moment stretched in the silence between them, "what happens if I can't? What if everything goes wrong?" *What if I'm not strong enough, clever enough to choose correctly? What if I fail in fighting the fate my father bargained for me?*

"They will rise from the undercity, spreading through the kingdom to gather sacrifice from the citizens of Inara, taking all they can in the name of magic. They will spend it like water, an endless well of energy at their disposal. Inara will fall. The world we know will be no more." He ran a thumb over her cheek. "You and I will be punished worst of all."

The seneschal had vowed not to lie to her. Sometimes, Nim thought maybe it would be easier if he could. Her voice was quiet and rough. "That's what I thought."

"You should go back to your room, my lady, unless you've made your decision about the ceremony."

That was truthful as well—she could tell that he did think she should go, but only because he was having trouble preventing himself from crossing a line with her standing in his private study.

Her voice remained low, only a breath of space between them as one of his hands rested over her hip and the other toyed with a loose lock of her dark hair. "You can't give me a secret passageway to your rooms and expect me not to use it."

His smile said he could and had, and Nim had the distinct impression that he would use any weapon in his arsenal to get her to decide quickly. She could not decide quickly, because it had been decided for her.

"You're right," she said, rising onto her toes to reach him. "I should definitely go." She brushed her lips over his in a long, lingering kiss that made her regret that she hadn't agreed, no matter what Stewart had warned, then drew back to say in a teasing tone, "I have work in the morning."

Warrick watched her as she turned and strode to the passageway, and as she glanced over her shoulder before stepping out, she knew for certain that his concern for her was separate from his desire to be her husband. She could feel that he wanted to keep her near him, to keep her safe, but not just for the protection the legal bonds afforded. Warrick wanted her at his side.

Of course he was tired of pushing away everything he came to care for, but she could sense that he was tired, too, of fighting his attachment to her. She wasn't certain it would have mattered —Nim had already come to realize that she couldn't let him go any more than she could Allister or Margery, but it was something else altogether to feel that surety from him and to know that she could trust him above all else. Her decision was made when it came to Warrick, as it had been the night she'd asked him if she could stay, but the word of the king was law. Once she agreed to a union against Stewart's wishes, she would be breaking that law in the very castle he ruled.

What a fool she would have to be, she mused, if she chose to turn two kingdoms against herself.

CHAPTER 5

The next morning, Nim was awoken by the bright light of a too-early sun as Maris yanked the curtains back on her bed. "Good morning, my lady," she offered with a cheerful smile.

"Oh, Maris," Nim said with a groan. "You're the morning sort."

The maid smiled. "Aye, my lady. Early to bed, early to rise." She tied the curtain back and snapped the edge of it straight. "Now, off to work today?"

"Yes, please. I've had all the idle time I can manage if you'll not let me sleep through it."

Maris chuckled. "Up, then, and let us get you sorted." She led her yawning charge to the vanity, where Maris served her strong tea and a handful of biscuits before moving to her back to untangle the mess of Nim's long dark hair. Her fingers wove skillfully through the locks, arranging them into a braid that she tucked and pinned securely at the base of her neck.

Maris seemed deft in all her tasks, with a sharp eye for detail. Nim hadn't a full-time maid since she was a girl, and she'd forgotten the depth of knowledge about their charges such a position afforded. Warrick trusted the woman, surely, or he would never have assigned her to Nim. But it would not be an easy thing to bare her private self so openly after years of hiding.

As she set the cup down, Nim's gaze caught on a pair of dark sapphire gems resting atop jewelry in a small porcelain dish. A spike of fear shot through her, and the cup tumbled, tea sloshing onto the vanity and into the dish. Her abrupt movement had tugged her braid from Maris's grip, and the maid was maneuvering dish and towel and all in her haste to prevent the spill from ruining more than it already had. She set the things in the basin, presumably to deal with at a later point, and Nim's mouth opened, but her protests fell short. She was being ridiculous, surely. There was no way the gems were the ones she'd feared. No way at all dark magic could reach her inside a king's castle and under Warrick's protection.

The maid was behind her again before Nim had fully decided whether to press the issue, prodding a last lock of hair into place. "There," Maris said. "All to rights." Her gaze turned to the mirror, catching Nim's eye. "Off to the wardrobe."

Nimona thought she managed to school her expression, but the corner of Maris's mouth tweaked, apparently assuming that her concern was regarding her new wardrobe. The woman crossed to a massive cabinet and drew open the finely carved doors. The interior was filled with gowns that shouldn't have had the proper time to be made, and Nim was hit again with the dizzying sensation of too much all at once.

Maris stepped to the side to allow a better view. "These are only to start. Alterations had to be made to accommodate the seneschal's wishes, but a full wardrobe will find its way to you shortly."

Nim gave the cabinet a narrow eye. She didn't imagine she would need much more than the dozen inside.

Maris tugged one hem forward to display the design. "For today, one of these." The long skirt was split down the front to reveal a pair of slim trousers underneath. Another outfit caught her eye, fitted trousers and a bodice with a long cape that attached over the shoulder to flow from around her back and arms to drape nearly to the floor. It was Nim's nighttime venturing wardrobe with society-appropriate shrouding—nearly appropriate, anyway. She'd yet to gauge the response of those who filled the halls.

"And for gatherings of the king's advisers." Maris gestured toward a half dozen formal gowns, rich fabrics with little frill, then gave Nim a knowing grin. "With these reserved for festivals and balls."

Nim stared at the finery, fully aware that her brow had knitted. "Will there be many balls and gatherings?"

Maris smoothed a palm over one fine dress as dark as a starless night. "Not that you will be required to attend, but a half dozen a year at least. There's the Festival of the Seasons, Soulsday, the Feast of the King..." She frowned, and Nim had the sense she'd not realized she was speaking aloud. "We don't celebrate Moontide any longer, not since the king's proclamation. I'll need to remember to not allow you a bit of silver then, should the king see you." She shook her head, snapping back to the posture of a lady's maid. "So," she asked, "do you have a preference?"

Nim nodded toward the nearest, trousers beneath the layer of skirt. "Thank you, Maris. I can dress myself, but I'll need direction to my new post."

"Wesley will fetch you. We're not to leave you adrift, my lady. Please call on us any moment you have a concern." Her words were so casually assured that Nim felt the tightness in her chest ease.

Maris laid the gown over a settee and retrieved a pair of tall boots from the wardrobe before securing the doors once more. "You'll be served a light meal midday, which I can have sent to your study. Or, should you prefer, you may take it in the garden. It promises to be a lovely day, the chill of springtide all but forgotten."

"That sounds wonderful. You have my gratitude."

"'Tis nothing," she assured. "I can only hope that you will soon find Inara Castle feels like home."

⁂

MARIS HAD TAKEN the basin with the jewels and sodden rags when she'd left, and a newly attired Nim was fidgety by the time Wesley finally arrived to escort her to her post. She could not seem to shake the sensation of fingers crawling over her, the unsettling familiarly of things that should have been unfamiliar. She was grateful to see him and to leave her room.

It was a short walk through lesser-used corridors, though the pair did pass a handful of courtiers and castle staff. None seemed to give notice to Nim's trousers, though to be fair, they were well hidden beneath the thin layer of skirt.

"Here we are, my lady," Wesley said, leading her into a massive library lit by a tall row of windows and littered with candelabra and sconces.

"It's lovely," she murmured before glancing at Wes. "Where is my workroom?"

Wesley smiled. "This. The assigned location for your new office. Do you like it?"

She nearly gaped at the expansive rows of shelves lined with books and safely tucked away from the ample sunlight and two large desks of the finest quality, each as wide as her bed. A cart of parchment and scrolls waited beside a table, which held inkwells and wax and supplies of the highest grade. "Maris said it was a study."

Wes chuckled. "A grand one, to be certain, but yes. I suppose it is." He watched her expression. "Warrick will be pleased it suits you."

"Suits me?" She shook her head, unable to take in all of it. "It is far beyond my needs."

"But not more than you deserve, I think." At Wesley's words, Nim's gaze snapped back to his. He shrugged. "I understand we've both been given graces, and there are many less fortunate. But Nim, this was your birthright. And it was taken from you by them."

Stolen by the Trust. She wasn't certain that was entirely true, though, because though Nim's freedom had been stolen, her father had willingly bargained away her future.

Wesley seemed to guess the direction of her thoughts. "All of it was in sacrifice to the kingdom, my lady. All so that this place" —he gestured around them—"could be safeguarded for the people of Inara, the people who built this kingdom in time before record." He took her hand in his, his scars hidden beneath thin black gloves. "And now, it is you who will protect it —protect us."

Nim's voice was weak. "You put too much faith in me, Wesley. It is the king who will protect Inara. With Warrick at his side."

Wesley's mouth tweaked into a lopsided grin as if against his will. "Aye, my lady." His finger tapped the ring that circled Nim's own. "And who will stand at Warrick's side?"

Her face went hot, and she had the startling urge to sit right where she stood. Fates, but she was a fool, time and again. Warrick was heir, not some courtier who might someday retire. He was to be king, and she—well, she had to have lost her mind to agree to marry him. "It's ridiculous," she argued. She really had not thought the scenario through. Surely, she'd planned to be dead by then, at the very least. "I can't contemplate such a thing. Wes, please do not make me."

He snickered. "As you wish, my lady. But I think you'll make a quite dashing queen."

Her gaze narrowed on him. "Dashing, is it? Are you working on my introduction?"

"Oh no, I've sorted that already," he said with all seriousness. He straightened. "Her Ladyship Nimona Weston, Royal Constable and Adviser to the Seneschal..." His brows knitted together. "Or will it be Nimona Spenser, then?"

"Please stop, Wesley. I feel as if I might be sick."

"It could be worse." He raised a shoulder in a shrug. "You at least have some chance of setting things to right."

Nim's heart squeezed. Wesley's parents had made sacrifices, as hers had, in the hopes that the boy would someday become a great swordsman. But he had been left with nothing but an aversion to blades, unable to wield the magic-bought sword which had cost those he loved their lives. It was the kind of perversion bargains usually brought, stealing away the very thing a person wanted in a way they didn't expect, a subversion of the terms. "Because of you," Nim said, "I am able to live. The sword they bargained for allowed me to best Calum. And you at my side was all that helped me through. This is ours, Wes. This chance belongs to both of us."

His hazel eyes came to hers. "I owe you for that as well." He held a gloved hand up to her. "It was Calum who wound these scars through my hands, Calum who stole my ability to use the sword. He's locked away now. Thanks to you, I feel safe even when Warrick is not at my side."

"Calum? He's who did that to you?"

Wes nodded. "After the bargain, when I was just a boy and my parents were gone, he tricked me, tore the sacrifice from me, and gave me nothing but pain in return. Warrick found out, thank the fates, and saved me from something worse. But what you did, Nim... none of us could have done that."

Us. "Wesley, are there others like you and me?"

His eyes darted toward the door. "I'm not supposed to talk about it, my lady. I'm sorry I brought it up. It's just that, well, I trust you. But there are things I should never say, no matter what. They aren't like us, the others who made sacrifices. Calum got to them first. All Warrick could do was save them from the undercity, from a cell where the magic might take hold. It was too late for them."

Warrick had taken ownership of their situations, Nim realized, as he'd done for Wesley and Nim. Those sacrifices had been made in his name, to secure an heir and save Inara when Warrick was the only surviving heir. He had tried to free them from Calum and from the Trust.

Nim truly did feel as if she might be sick. It had been Calum all along, not the magic. Every bad thing she'd ever felt had come from Calum and the queen. She shook off the shiver that trailed down her spine. "You're right, Wes. There are things to keep put away." She squeezed his hand briefly. "Thank you for trusting me."

He seemed to shake himself as well but quickly returned to his duties to draw a letter from inside his robes. "Warrick has sent a message for you. Instructions for your tasks." As Nim took it, Wes added, "I'll see you tomorrow to escort you to Hearst manor and to call on Lady Margery."

"I look forward to it," she told him. "And I'm certain both have prepared a delightful selection of cakes for our visit."

"You recognize my heart, Lady Weston." He gave her a final crooked grin before he bowed and turned to stride from the room.

Nim took in the massive space once more, turning slowly to gaze over every surface of the room. It was too much, all of it. And yet, warm in her hand was a missive from the man who was second only to the king.

She stared down at the letter, running a finger over its fine wax seal. Within the seal was the magic that was Warrick, protecting the message in the way he had protected Wesley, the way he had protected her, a magic that felt safe and warm and right in all the ways Calum's had felt so wrong. The seal cracked easily, revealing Warrick's elegant hand.

My lady, it said, the sentiment somehow more personal than it had ever been. The message included a detailed list of instructions for her post and, to her great surprise, that should she desire to follow up on information found during her research, she would be afforded the ability to call in noblemen and commoners alike for questioning. She moved to the nearest desk and sat heavily in a chair. Fates save her, but Warrick had given her a station that granted her real power. It seemed vaguely reckless, but she supposed it offered more protection than simply hiding her away. Only a brazen fool would have risked gaining the ire of the seneschal, let alone that she could make any courtier's life as difficult as she pleased, given the proper motives.

Only a day before, a king had warned Nimona that one misstep would be the death of her, and yet, she felt the safest she'd ever been. Calum was locked away in the dungeons of Inara Castle, under guard and bound by blood and magic, and not only had she been returned to the castle in which she'd been born, but she had gained a station far beyond her imaginings... because of Warrick.

Nim was constable. She wasn't certain she was up to the task, but if any one thing might be able to save her, it was knowledge of what the magic was and how it worked. She needed to answer the question that had plagued her since she was a child: *Why does the magic want me?*

CHAPTER 6

By late afternoon, Nim sat before the largest of her new study's desks, its surface blanketed in ledgers and scrolls. There was far more information than she'd anticipated—insight the likes of which she'd never had access to before, no matter how many hours she'd spent researching assigned marks for the Trust, too many missives and accounts the king's guard had deemed suspicious. She couldn't say that they were wrong, though. Every seized document was tied to unusual occurrences similar in description to tactics used by the Trust. But Nim did not sense magic in them. Whatever illicit ventures the messages might have aided, they had not been sealed with blood in the way the most incriminating documents were.

She made a note to inquire about two royal posts she was not familiar with and backgrounds on several lords and ladies mentioned in a particularly confounding missive. She'd been out of good society for far too long to know everyone, but she understood how court maneuvering worked. She understood the types of citizens the Trust would target, and since the last moon, since meeting Warrick, she was beginning to understand why.

The Trust and their accountants were working hard to

subvert whatever bargains and rules tied them from acting above ground and in Inara. They wanted the kingdom more than anything, freedom to steal without repercussion the sacrifices required to pay magic's toll. She lay down her quill to rub her temple and sensed something shift near the edge of the room.

Nim startled, reaching automatically to her thigh, but she was weaponless. Her breath rushed out of her at the sight of Warrick, though she wasn't certain how long he'd been watching from the shadows. "You have to stop sneaking up on me."

He gave her a smile that said it was not his fault that she had been so engrossed in her work that she forgot her surroundings. She narrowed her gaze on him but gave it up for blinking away the echo of lines caused by staring at so much print.

"Overworking yourself on the first day, my lady?" He came to lean on the desk beside her, so tall that she had to shift back in her chair to stare up at him.

"There is a lot to go through. And I'm not used to being idle."

He eyed her attempt at surreptitiously stretching a hand. "Maris tells me you've worked through lunch."

"Thank you for alerting me that she's a traitor to my secrets."

Warrick smirked, but his gaze trailed from her hand down the length of her skirt, split as it was to reveal her slim pants. He reached forward, lifting a bit of the material aside as if to inspect it, but Nim wasn't fooled. "So you've come to vet my uniform, my lord?"

His green eyes rose to meet hers, an intimation rolling off of him that made her warm all the way through. "By all means, do report for dress inspection, my lady."

She stared at him for a long moment, the heat only ebbing when he held out a hand.

"I do understand that you are not normally idle," he said, "so I would like to escort you to the gardens for a stroll. It will not do you well to spend too many hours crooked over ledgers."

Nim placed her hand in his, their fingers bare aside from the thin silver band that circled hers. "I suppose you would know something about that." Her voice was more timid than usual, but Warrick had a way of stealing from her the very stubbornness she'd always relied on to get through.

His thumb slid over the back of her hand, and Nim had the sense that it was the last touch he would be allowed, since they were leaving the privacy of her room. The intimation said that he did not relish the idea, and she found she didn't, either. She stood, pressing his hand to the desk beside him as she leaned forward, caging him not unlike the way he'd done to her the first time they'd met. An indecent grin slid across Warrick's lips as she peered down at him.

"Trapped," she whispered.

Warrick only hummed in agreement. As the sound rumbled through her, she could feel that he was remembering, too, how he'd watched her scale his desk and then the feeling when they were near to one another. Trapped, he seemed to think, was not a strong enough word for what he was.

She eased closer to steal a kiss, his mouth soft and warm as the hand she'd not pinned slid to her waist. She was going to have to marry him, the king's warning be damned, or at some point, they would be caught in just such a situation—unfit behavior for agents of the crown. She was going to have to find a way to break free from the ties to magic before Stewart or anyone else discovered her secret.

She nipped Warrick's lip then drew away, flipping the edge of her skirt to straighten the fabric. "Now," she said, "that stroll."

After a quiet walk through a private garden near the center of the castle grounds, Nim had returned to her study to find that a late lunch had been set out for her, along with a new collection of documents and scrolls. She did feel better after the air and a bit of sun, but she could not deny that Warrick's presence had done the most for her mood. She settled in to return to what was by all appearances going to be an endless task and found that she did not dislike the idea. Research had always suited her, and the possibility of learning more about those around her and better understanding the dangers the Trust presented would afford her more security than she'd ever known.

When a quiet knock sounded at the door hours later, Nim glanced up and blinked her weary eyes at Maris.

"My lady," she said. "I've come to drag you back to your rooms. You should prep to go down for supper, unless you prefer to stay in again."

Nim returned her quill to its place and stretched her fingers, imagining a formal dinner with the lords and ladies of court. No, she didn't think she would be eager to join them anytime soon, and Warrick's post kept him occupied well into the evening hours. "I believe I'll take dinner in my rooms, if it's no bother."

"Of course not." Maris's tone gave no impression whatsoever, but the small tip to the edge of her mouth seemed to imply that Nim had made a solid choice.

As Nim stood, her gaze caught on the edge of a document beneath the stack, one she'd not yet gotten to. She tugged it free of the others, running a finger over parchment that was strangely familiar. Her flesh brushed against the ink, written in a heavy, slanted hand, and Nim jerked her finger back as if bitten. The words seemed harmless enough, but in them was a recognizable magic. Unease skittered over her, but Calum was locked away beneath the castle. Then again, if he had woven his magic into the document, he would have done so before he was captured.

He could not hurt her any longer.

She left the parchment where it lay to be passed on for further inspection and turned to meet Maris. They walked at a measured pace through the corridors. Nim was starting to become familiar with the layout of her new rooms, which overlapped the remembered routes of her childhood. She wondered where Warrick had been when she was a child, if they had both resided inside the castle then. She would never have known who he was, given the secret her mother and father had kept. It was probably ill-advised to ask whether the head of the Trust had delivered him to the king's doorstep when he was a babe or if he had been with his mother longer.

Nim shuddered at the memory of her encounter with the head of the Trust and the depth of power she had felt then. It seemed impossible to imagine her anger or cruelty when even her pleasure at seeing Nim had been impossibly torturous. It had been so long ago, and yet, the horror in her father's face as he turned to find her, barefoot and slight in the massive chamber that held a queen... that image had never left her. It was the first time she'd known real fear, the first time she'd had a true understanding of that other world, the first time the magic had touched her.

"My lady," Maris said, turning to stand at the open door to her suite.

Nim shoved the thoughts away and locked them into a box in her mind, aware that she should keep a tighter rein. There were too many memories in the castle, too many ways she might slip.

She sighed as she strode across the room and unfastened the closures on her jacket. Tossing it over a chair, she stood in the light before her writing desk. A bit of metal on the quill shone with reflected light from the lowering sun, and she stared at it quizzically. She was certain the metal had been silver before, but maybe that had been the adornments on the quill in her other room. Behind her, the space was empty, Maris having gone about preparations for the evening's meal. Nim's gaze caught on the panel that hid the secret corridor then grazed the mantel, the table, the remaining doors.

Shaking off her disquiet, she made her way to the basin to wash her hands and found that soap and lemon had been left in a delicately carved dish. The best practice to ward off any permanent ink stains was that her wardrobe was already black, but she scrubbed and dried her fingers. Her gaze lingered on the silver ring. The awful truth stared back at her.

No matter how much she might have wished it otherwise, Nim would have to decline Warrick's plans. There was no way she could set herself up to be queen. Even if that day was far off and unimaginable, the risk was there. Stewart was right—someone tied to magic by bargain had no business near anyone who might take the throne. And Warrick, well, he was already a risk. If the public found out he was son of the head of the Trust, there was no telling what might come of Inara. It had been a tightly held secret for a reason, and all that was holding the kingdom together was that the Trust played a long game. They had pieces remaining in play.

Nim had removed Calum, but he had not been their only marker. Wesley had said the Trust had someone in place, should the king not produce an heir, and—fates forbid something happen to Warrick—that a council would decide on a new king from among one of the older lines. The Trust had a man in position who would be king, tied to their magic and under their command. Nim did not know precisely who that man was, but she intended to find out.

"My lady." Maris's voice cut through the thought, and Nim turned to find that the maid had already set dinner and was waiting for Nim's approval.

"Thank you," Nim said. "Please, sit with me and eat." Maris started to protest, but Nim waved it off. "You have to do as I've asked. You've already admitted as much, and besides, I'll never get through so much food alone." She crossed to stare at the spread. "Honestly, it's almost insulting that they think I would."

Maris pressed her lips together hard but managed to suppress a smile.

It might someday be nice to be able to catch a smile so easily amidst the many rules of propriety, but the idea made Nim miss her steadfast valet even more. She was grateful that she would see him on the morrow. Allister had been her only constant for so long that it was hard not to look for him each time she woke, when dinner was called, or when a message arrived. Her candles were still lit and her clothes pressed, and Nim was not without someone at every turn, but she felt his loss in each of those things nonetheless.

She settled onto a chair, snatching the napkin from Maris as she prepared to snap it in place, and ordered the woman to sit. No matter what else, Nim had much to be grateful for. Whatever the Trust had taken from her, whatever they planned to do, Nim wouldn't have to face it alone. Not any longer.

CHAPTER 7

Nim jolted upright in bed, choking on the phantom sensation of long fingers wrapped around her neck. Sweat dampened her shift, and the blankets were like a tangle of writhing serpents around her limbs. She jerked free, nearly falling in her haste to escape, her feet landing heavily on the cool floor of her room as her fingers raked the bare skin of her throat. She stared through the darkness, searching for the source of the lingering magic snaking over her skin. The muddled feeling of having woken when she'd not meant to fall asleep faded like mist in the sunrise, and she drew in a sharp breath. On the pillow beside her rested two dark gemstones.

It had not been a dream that had woken her but something far, far worse. Nim cursed and yanked a dark robe over her shift. She shoved her feet into slippers and crossed to a low table. The steel shears were gone. She grabbed a long, solidly-built candle-holder instead, gripping it tightly enough that her knuckles went white. A rustling sound came from the other side of her door-way, but Nim did not wait to see if Maris had stirred. She snatched a small taper, which she lit from the tinderbox, then strode straight to the hidden panel, slipping into the dark corridor with no more than a single flame to light her way.

She did not turn on the path that was familiar, her feet instead drawing her toward the slithering magic that had invaded her peace. It was not that she wanted to reward him or to let him think he'd somehow won, but that she needed to be sure. She had to see with her own eyes that it hadn't been real and that Calum was indeed still in his cell.

The passageway was narrow, the air stale, but all she could feel was the draw of magic. She followed it through the corridors. The first door she tried was blocked by something immovable, but the second opened into an empty hall behind a heavy tapestry. Barely managing to escape with her flame intact, she checked the halls for any sign of the guard then strode toward a darkened stairwell, its steps twisting down through air that was too damp and too cool against the exposed skin of her throat. She drew the robe tighter around her neck.

Two men stood posted at the hall before the dungeons, but that was not where Nim felt the magic's draw. She crept through the labyrinth of corridors to a passage even farther down. It was windowless and dark. Her flame barely illuminated her way, and Nim startled when a staff shot across the path before her.

She drew back, sucking in air as her eyes adjusted. Nim shifted the flame of her taper, hoping the candlestick she brandished in her other hand as a potential weapon was obscured by dim light and the material of her robes. A guard gave a plainly disapproving look to Nim's escapade. There was a soft noise somewhere behind her, but she wasn't certain how many more might be standing in wait. Calum was close—she could feel it. Shifting her light, she took in the second guard's face. His expression was decidedly worse.

"Lady Weston."

His voice was deep, and though it was the first time she'd heard it, she knew just who he was, the guard she'd knocked from the wagon with Wes's magic-bought sword. It was less likely that it was bad luck and more likely that he'd been assigned watch in a dark dungeon precisely because he'd failed to keep her under control.

She straightened. "Excellent. You know who I am." His resulting smirk and a quick assessment of her situation resolved any hope she might have harbored that she'd be able to sneak by. She might have tossed her candle toward them and ducked into the shadows, but the door would be secured, and she'd no time to pick a lock before they found her again. Even the magic-bought sword, should she have had it, wouldn't have given her the time she needed.

"Yes, my lady, I know who you are," the guard said. "And I have express orders not to let you pass."

"I see," Nim said coolly, the candlestick she was wielding like a mace heavy in her hand.

The first guard's gaze narrowed. She cleared her throat.

A thick silence followed as she considered her next move.

Then a new voice came from the darkness—Warrick's. "Let her pass."

Nim's shoulders stiffened, but she managed not to turn around. She felt Warrick move closer behind her, and though she was certain his face would hold its usual sober-as-a-seneschal expression, she was surprised he sent her nothing more than a vague intimation about confronting Calum in not much more than her shift.

She bit back any remark she might have made, keeping her gaze steady on the guard. Warrick would have had no way of knowing she'd come, no time to have been alerted, surely, and that only firmed her resolve to see Calum with her own eyes. Warrick must have felt something too.

The guard moved to the massive doorway and unlocked a complicated mechanism that the darkness made it difficult for her to make out well. The heavy slab door opened into another corridor, and magic swelled from within, beckoning her.

She resisted the urge to back away. Certain Warrick had noticed the flinch, even from behind her, she walked forward without glancing back. She felt him following, but he stuck to the shadows, letting her stride toward another foolish thing at her own pace.

There were no other doors and no hidden chambers or additional passageways, only a large archway carved into the stone, latticed with heavy iron bars. Beyond it, in the darkness, Nim felt something wicked from a shadowy shape.

"My lady." Calum's voice was silky, unconcerned, as if he'd not been trapped in a cell.

Light flared as several torches came to life behind him, and she flinched, but apparently, he'd seen well enough to recognize her in the dark.

Calum leaned casually against the back wall of his cell in the same clothes he had been wearing when he was captured. He was nothing like how she'd imagined him, not cowed in the least. And yet, it had only been days, no matter that her world had since been turned upside down. Maybe after a few months or a year, he would begin to show the wear a dark part of her needed to see.

Calum's lips tipped up at the edges in a nasty smile. "Did you miss me?"

His whisper tickled unpleasantly over her skin, and her fingers tightened on the candlestick waiting in her best fighting hand. She did not answer, not sure what she had been so eager to say. The point was only to see him, she supposed, to know that he was there and that she was safe.

But Calum straightened to saunter toward her, and she felt nothing of the sort. He came to a stop before the bars, not touching the metal but hovering excruciatingly near. He had asked if she'd missed him, but the intimations he sent her said how much he had thought of seeing her and what he had imagined doing to her the moment he was free. Because he would get free, those imaginings seemed to promise, and so, so soon.

Nim gritted her teeth. Calum laughed. "I know why you are here, my lady." His dark gaze roamed the darkness beyond her then returned with no mention of the magic Nim had felt or the personal items that had been tampered with in her rooms. "But how could I do such a thing, when you bound me yourself?" He held up his wrists, unbound as they were, and purred, "Here I am, at your mercy." His tone was sickly sweet, and though his words vowed that he was bound, the pleasure that twisted his lips said something else entirely.

Her stomach swam. He meant whatever dark secret that danced around the edges of his intimations. Calum knew he would be free and would come for her, just as he said.

Nim stumbled back, but Warrick moved out of the darkness, a silent threat radiating from him as he stopped at Nimona's side then slipped a warm hand over the small of her back to steady her.

Calum's gaze slid over them both, mischief glittering in eyes as dark as onyx. An intimation rose again, one that promised that Warrick would have to watch whatever was done to the lady Nimona.

Warrick's jaw went tight, but Calum's smirk seemed only to beg his brother to harm him, to break the terms of their agreement so that Calum could be free.

Beside Nim, Warrick's response was spoken softly but menacingly. "I wouldn't dream of touching you." He handed Nim a short dagger, the threat in his gesture clear. He wouldn't have to touch Calum himself, not when anyone else could torture him at their will.

A strange sensation swelled through Nim as her fingers closed tighter around the dagger. She didn't recall the candlestick being torn from her grip, but it was gone, replaced with a weapon that was warm and tingling with magic. It was well made, very much the size and weight of the one she'd carried for years, but a bit more solid, its handle carved with delicate scrollwork reminiscent of vines, the material far finer than any she'd ever held. It was woven with Warrick's magic, but she wasn't certain exactly what that might buy her.

She stared up at him, a question in her gaze. Voice low, he only murmured, "A wedding present."

Something dark swelled from Calum, its bite sharp and deep, but when Nim's gaze shot to him, whatever rage he'd let slip was suddenly tied within him, hidden from her entirely.

Nim wondered if he'd been able to keep it out of her reach even when he'd been so brutally angry all along. Her memory of the small room deep within the undercity rose unbidden, with Calum holding her down, whispering cruel promises into her ear.

Her grip tightened around the dagger. Calum truly had hated her, maybe as much as she'd come to hate him. She understood suddenly—from the beginning, he'd known what her contract entailed and that no matter what he wanted, the head of the Trust had tied Nimona Weston to Inara's fate and to Warrick, because the queen intended to use him and to gain Inara—but not for Calum. He had not gone after only Nim. He had gone for the others, Wesley had said, everyone who had been tied to bargains by the king's men in their desire to save the kingdom.

It was not just her and not just once. Calum had been calculating, stacking the odds in his favor. He was playing a bigger game than petty revenge.

Calum was heir to the Trust, but by the grace of the fates, he was bound by Nim's terms. Even so, she could feel the remembered magic pressing against her in the darkness not so long ago, the torture of his intimations as he leaned near.

"I own you," he'd whispered against her ear.

Nim would not give in to the darkness that wanted to say it back to him, even as he was trapped within magical bonds and behind iron bars. She would not stab him. The best punishment would be to let him live, to force him to endure. Calum couldn't read her mind, but she let him see it in her smile. He would never own anyone again.

WARRICK WAS silent as they left the cell. He said nothing at all and sent no intimations on the long walk back to his rooms. Once they stood in the center of his study, Nim turned to face him, desperate for some reason she could not quite pin down. "I needed to see him. To see for myself that he was there." Bound, trapped, no longer a threat but real and solid in his cell.

Warrick leaned back against his desk, crossing his arms over his broad chest. "Why?"

Nim searched his face. His expression was calm even as something roiled beneath. He clearly didn't question her motivations to see Calum but wondered why she hadn't come to him instead. Nim had known something was wrong. Warrick had felt it, the same as she had. Like a fool, she'd run straight to Calum to play into his hands. Had it been a trap, she would have fallen for it.

And all she had to do was come to Warrick's rooms.

A muscle ticked in his jaw. "The safest place for you is at my side."

Truth. The same as everything Warrick said to her, and not simply because of his vow. He wanted her safe, protected. Nim was the one constantly throwing herself into the path of danger.

She frowned, pressing down the apology that started to bubble up. She owed no apologies. And even if she had, it was not what he wanted. He wanted... something else. She could feel it.

His gaze raked over her as if checking to be certain she was unharmed. He hadn't liked seeing her so close to Calum and clearly hadn't liked that she'd planned to confront him alone. Her fingers played nervously on the hilt of the dagger. She moved closer, stopping just out of reach of him.

"Thank you," she said. She was fairly certain that she meant far more than the dagger, but it was a start.

He dipped his chin. "Don't use it on my guards."

Nim pressed her lips to hold down a smile. "I said I was sorry about that." His intimations slipped just enough to remind her of the grip she'd held on that candlestick. She cleared her throat. "Wesley said something that has me thinking."

Warrick's expression shifted, probably given the sudden swing in the conversation. One side of his brow rose. It made him painfully tempting.

"About your last name," she explained. He reached across the distance, tugging her close. She gave him a small smile. "I suppose it isn't truly yours, given the secret." Nim had a vague recollection of a long-ago officer of the court with the family name Spenser, but she wasn't certain if the king had meant to hide Warrick as the man's son or some other, more distant relative.

"I don't suppose I ever expected someone to take it." His voice was soft, contemplative, and sent a shiver over her skin entirely unlike the unpleasant magic from earlier. Warrick's magic was a delicious sort of tension, and the more she felt of it, the more she wanted of it. His eyes rose to hers. "You may keep your father's name, love." *As long as I have you.*

Nim swallowed hard. His intimations had returned, and she'd been entirely correct about what he was holding back. Warrick knew the Trust was toying with them, and he didn't hide that he wanted nothing more than Nim at his side. He couldn't leave the decision to her any longer, not when she was at risk. He would have to bind her to him, to reveal precisely what they were up against. He needed to do it now. He needed to have the thing done.

She shook her head, nearly overwhelmed by the force of his intimations. The king had said he would see her killed. And Calum, well, his response had been even worse. They would incite the wrath of Warrick's father and his mother—the king of Inara and the head of the Trust. It felt like another fool thing, and yet, of all the fool things she'd done, choosing Warrick was the only one that truly made sense or made her feel safe. He was the only one she had ever imagined making sacrifices for— Warrick, who had never asked a sacrifice of her at all.

She leaned into him, setting her dagger on the desk beside him to plant her palms against his chest. He was wearing only a thin shirt, and beneath it were scars born of sacrifices he'd made for others.

"Yes," she whispered. "Fates save us both from the consequences, but yes. Let us be married."

CHAPTER 8

Nim had returned to her room in the small hours before dawn, her mind reeling with the plans Warrick had laid out. They would meet the following night after his duties as seneschal were complete to hold a ceremony before a magistrate and witness, and then, once she and Warrick were bound by law, the king would not be able to act against her without bringing scrutiny upon Warrick. Until then, Nim would not be able to breathe a word of it to anyone. So come morning, she would carry on with her visits to Allister and Margery as if nothing at all were amiss. It would require more untruths, but there was not much else to be done if she intended to stay alive.

She shook the nervous energy from her hands as she crossed the room then froze as her curtain-draped bed came into view. She had forgotten what had sent her running in her haste to find Calum and the planning that followed. Her feet moved slower, and her palm found the dagger she'd stashed in the pocket of her robe.

Standing before the bed she'd so recently escaped, Nim stared down at the pillow. On it, beside where her head had rested, lay two tiny jewels. No part of her was fool enough to think she should touch them, but the draw to magic never made sense. Her fingers stretched across the linens, barely brushing the sapphires before the magic within pricked her flesh. She snatched her hand back, stumbling away from the bed.

It had felt of Calum's magic, dark, venomous, and familiar in a way that made her ill.

He was in the dungeon, alone in a cell, and yet, the matching gems to the ones she'd stolen to bind him—the ones Warrick had used to seal the new contract—lay on her pillow. The emeralds had been pried free from the three-headed snake that adorned Calum's door, and he'd hidden them with the contract he'd used to trick Nim. But the door's sapphires had been intact the last she'd seen them.

The emeralds had belonged to the center snake, its eyes as green as Warrick's. A sick feeling swelled through Nim as she recalled the other two carved serpents. The first had eyes of dark onyx, as black as Calum's in the shadows. And the last, smaller serpent had held the sapphires, the serpent whose mouth was wide to reveal a set of lethal fangs. Her fingers curled into her palm as she remembered how the magic had drawn her, how the entire door had seemed to writhe beneath her touch, beckoning her. Recollections of the sensation inside the darkened corridor on her way to find Warrick followed—fingers trailing her skin, though she'd found nothing behind her.

Someone had been inside her rooms.

"My lady."

Nim nearly jumped from her skin at the sound of Maris's voice. Heart pounding, she spun, dagger in one hand and the other pressed to her chest. "Maris. I'm sorry, I—"

What, she didn't know. Warrick had kept his secrets. He had vowed not to lie to her, but there were things he was bound not to tell. Nim had discovered that Calum was his brother and realized that the two shared a mother. But there was more that she had not considered, more that could do her in.

"My lady," Maris said again, something careful and cagey in her tone.

Nim lowered the dagger to her side. "I only had a fright," she answered. "I'm... it will be fine." She shook herself, straightening her shoulders as she turned to face Maris fully. "I'm afraid it's too late for me to return to sleep now. Perhaps an early breakfast before we're off to visit the manor and Lady Margery?"

Maris nodded and, if wary, still turned to go about the business of preparing for the day.

⁂

NIM DRESSED in one of the simpler gowns but strapped the dagger into a sheath on her thigh. She felt more confident with it, even though using a magical dagger on anyone, Trust associate or otherwise, would likely see her hanged. There were laws in Inara and laws within the Trust. Neither showed favor to someone like Nimona.

In short order, she'd managed to down a few bites of food and had walked with Maris through the courtyard in order to occupy herself outside the room. She was grateful she would not have to go back and that come evening, she would be staying with Warrick in his rooms. When Wesley finally came to fetch her, the night's events and lack of sleep had worn her down.

"Would you like to go another day?" Wes asked, concern evident in his hazel eyes.

She patted his arm. "I wouldn't want to miss this chance to see our friends, but thank you. I'm sure my enthusiasm will rally once we reach the manor."

He smiled. "Tea and cakes."

"Indeed," she said.

A pair of castle guards stood in the corridor, and Wes leaned in to whisper that it was only a precaution. She wasn't certain how much of her overnight adventure Warrick had relayed to Wes, but she supposed the additional protection would not hurt. The set of worries she'd grown used to had shifted into an unfamiliar reality. The guards were only part of it. She was an officer of the court, after all. Things had changed.

They were escorted to a waiting carriage, where the guards mounted a pair of stout black horses to follow. Wes had always walked to the manor, as had Nim, and a carriage would only have drawn attention they didn't need. Nim suspected it had more to do with her post and that she was to be installed as a respected lady of society than anything else.

The ride through the streets of Inara was short, the cobblestones smooth beneath the carriage wheels, and the citizens gracious enough to make way for the king's colors. When they arrived at Hearst Manor, they were greeted by a footman Nim did not recognize.

He dropped into a deep bow then raised his hand to assist her from the carriage without a word. Wesley followed, his gaze uncharacteristically cautious before he smiled at Nim and gave her his arm. An unfamiliar guard opened the door to Hearst, and they were led to the sitting room, where Alice and Allister waited.

Nim's chest eased in a sigh as she saw them, and she crossed the space before either had managed to get a proper greeting out. But as she reached for Allister, she caught sight of a long bruise that crossed his brow, a mottled purple band the precise width of Calum's cane. A sound resembling a wounded animal came out of her, and Allister took her hand.

"My lady," he said, nothing like distress in his tone. "All is well."

Nim pinched her eyebrows, and her gaze snapped to Alice, the sudden, sickening recollection of cracking bone making Nim want to retch. The girl's eyes were wide, but it appeared her concern was only for Nim. Reaching forward to brush a gentle finger over the girl's cheek, Nim did her best to hold back tears. Along Alice's hairline was a colorful palette of bruises, and her neck was covered in scratches and scrapes.

"I'm sorry," Nim choked out. "I never should have—"

"My lady." Alice's voice was sharp, cutting through whatever Nim had meant to say. "It's not proper to carry on in such a manner." Nim's mouth came open, but Alice gave a quick shake of her head. "We here at Hearst Manor are in the king's employ, your ladyship, and as such, I am obliged to remind you of the pecking order."

Nim blinked.

Allister's mouth went tight, but he managed not to break into what Nim imagined was a delightful smile. His grip on Nim's hand tightened almost imperceptibly. "Alice has been investigating the proper procedures of her new station, as she is well pleased to have been awarded the position by order of the king."

Alice leaned forward to whisper, "They sent the king's *personal* physician for us." Her eyes had gone impossibly wider, glinting with conspiratorial awe.

"Aye," Nim said, her voice a low vow. "You *are* very important to the king. Both of you." She felt Allister's dark eyes on her but couldn't meet his gaze without cascading into tears.

"Sit, my lady. Let us relish in the honor of serving tea to an agent of the kingdom. Do tell, what is the title of your new post?" He drew her onto the chaise beside him, and Alice snapped a gesture toward Wesley, commanding he be honored as well. He complied with a grin, spouting his practiced introduction even as his gaze flicked to her as if to assure himself that *Her Ladyship Nimona Weston, Royal Constable and Adviser to the Seneschal* was not about to crumble.

The hours sped past, and Nim understood in the depths of her heart that Allister did not fault her for anything that had happened. He had been at the very least aware of the gentleman Hearst's dealings with the Trust before she'd even come along. As his valet, Allister would have seen far too much and been far too close to whatever trouble Hearst had tangled himself in. There was nothing to be done to save the man. Besides, Nim had been so lost then. She'd been thrown into the home of her mark, forced by the Trust to be hosted in the very manor they had reclaimed from him. Nim had felt untethered and without hope but determined to fight despite it all.

Allister had done what he could to help her, but his hands had been tied. They had both known better than to speak of what had happened to the master of the house. Because speaking of the Trust was a certain way to end up killed, come one thing or another.

Nimona and Wesley were reluctant to leave the company of Allister and Alice, but Margery awaited a visit as well. With promises to return soon, they departed the manor and resumed the carriage to make the short trip to her friend's family home. Wesley retrieved the gift they'd brought for her from beneath the seat and was toying with the wrapping's trim when the horses screamed. He and Nim jolted alert, eyes darting forward to find the cause of the earsplitting sound as a covey of birds took flight around their transport.

The carriage had stopped abruptly, and the world outside went suddenly too silent, too still. Nim rushed to the door, jerking free of Wesley's hand as he tried to stop her, and alighted to the street. Despite the flock that had risen, around her lay the bodies of a dozen birds, lifeless, feathers unmoving in still air, noiseless in the unnatural hush. She felt Wesley move behind her, but her eyes had found the horse at the front of the carriage. It had fallen to the ground, bound in the harness. The second was invisible beyond the carriage and driver, but it, too, had gone silent.

Time had seemed to still, but it couldn't have been more than a moment, a single breath once Nim had moved. An echo of sound far off in the city reached her just as the drum of hoofbeats charged behind her, and she was being swept up by one of the guards who'd followed the carriage. Wes's grip tugged free as she was hauled away, and behind her, she saw that the second guard was reaching to drag him onto his horse. As her senses snapped back, Nim grabbed hold of the guard who held her, dragging her legs around the mount to secure herself as they raced through the streets.

If magic had swelled through the city, Nim had not felt it, but nothing else would so suddenly strike so many beasts at once. Allister had given her a handful of tonics, small glass bottles she'd dropped into her pocket to stash in her room. She scrambled to reach one, hands trembling. No one who had anything at all to lose was fool enough to attack a king's carriage.

CHAPTER 9

They made it just three streets before magic stung Nim's skin, sharp and hot, along with the sense that they'd only just managed the short distance for the chase. They were caught or being toyed with. If the horses had been dropped, it could have just as easily happened to the guards. But no, she remembered, Wesley had received a boon from the sacrifice Warrick had made—no one but Warrick could touch the boy with magic.

Their attacker had wanted them separated. Nim's gaze shot behind her, searching for Wes, but the horse beneath her stumbled forward, the guard she clung to powerless to stop the animal's fall. As the ground rushed toward them, the guard swung Nim away from the beast with one hand, his other raising his sword in preparation to fight. He would not win. She could feel it.

Her hands slammed against her temples, and she stumbled, the idea that the guard would be overtaken stabbing into her mind. It was not her own. It was an intimation, dark and sharp and too eager to make itself at home in her head.

Wes cried her name, and Nim forced her eyes open as the horse groaned and tried to regain its feet beside them. The guard had hold of her, keeping her out of reach from the struggling animal and tucked behind him, blade at the ready as he scanned the clearing for the source of the attack. A cold wind snapped through the street, where they were trapped in the too-narrow space between rows of buildings, too far from Wes and the other guard. Not a single soul stood streetside, no onlookers or sounds of panic, nothing but the hammering of Nim's heart.

And then she felt the sensation of fingers crawling over her skin, the awareness of something *other*. She turned to run toward Wesley, but it was too late. The magic closed around her, her neck in a vise made of nothing material, nothing she could claw at or fight. It lifted her from the ground, her feet dragging across the stones before they dangled above. Her hands came automatically to paw at her throat, but like in her room before, her fingers found only air. With her voice stolen and her breath coming in thin gasps, Nim found Wesley, who was caught in the arms of a pair of Trust accountants, horror and regret in his wide eyes. They couldn't use magic on him, but they didn't need to. They only needed to hold him there, apart from Nim and unable to protect her.

Wes shouted again as the sound of heavy, booted footsteps approached, but even if he managed to escape, Wes and their guard would be too slow. The man who had orchestrated Nim's capture was not playing by any rules.

He had her. There was nothing she could do. Nim was slammed to the ground a moment before more accountants took her arms. She jerked and fought, but they outsized her by half. And it would not be a fair fight, not when they loved nothing more than blood, not when her suffering would only feed their desire, their magic.

It didn't stop her from trying. She rammed her slippered foot into one of her captors as her other leg found purchase, using their grip on her for leverage as she tried to spin a kick into the second man. He was too fast, her strike missed, and she was pulled harder between them before they pressed closer with magic, crushing her chest even as they bound her feet from moving.

Unable to so much as scream, Nim was hauled from the street, the vile curses she wanted to spit stolen with her air. They rushed through an alley, her chest a thousand knives of pain, her body thrashing against restraints of magic as the men dragged her farther from Wes and the guards, away from anything safe. She could not think, could not focus, could obey nothing but the violent need to draw breath. Her thrashing became weak, her vision darkening. Then she was slammed against the ground, and cool stone struck her cheek.

NIM'S CHEST felt suddenly run through with a sword of fire, but her body was cold with sweat as it pressed into the solid stone beneath her. For a moment, head spinning, she was sure she was alone, trapped in the dark, that she'd been thrown into a cell beneath the earth. But it was worse, far worse.

Up, a voice commanded in her head. *Stand and face me.*

Nim retched onto the floor and had the sense it was not the first time she had since she'd been captured. She rolled to her back, dragging in breath, trying to force the dizziness to settle so she might find her bearings, but the magic swelled around her, undeniable proof that she'd been dragged into the undercity, deep within the catacombs that housed the Trust. Her hand found something warm and wet on the floor, and she flinched as her eyes finally focused on the flickering glow of firelit trenches and the dark stone of the undercity cells.

The brief thought that she might be thrown into one of those cells was gone before it could take root. Whatever the Trust had planned didn't involve simply locking her up.

She had not woken alone.

Nim pushed to her feet, wincing and pressing her eyes closed against a last wave of dizziness before she found her place. Allister's tonics had saved her, but the magic was still too strong.

She stood before a line of cells, their entrances low enough that they might have been made for creatures, not men, the iron bars revealing nothing but shadow beyond. The cells were never lit inside, so if anyone waited in their depths, they surely shied away from the flame, unable to watch. The accountants who'd dragged her there were gone, and Nim stood alone in a tunnel as finely crafted as the halls above. *Not alone*, some part of her warned, but it was far too late to heed the urge to run.

In the shadow of a doorway, a figure shifted into view, rolling lazily toward her with a shoulder rested against the wall. He was tall and lean, his form more graceful than spindly, but she could tell in just one move that he was agile, dangerous. His brow rose on one side, a sort of challenge, but Nim held her ground. It took everything not to allow herself to step back, but she understood precisely how much he would enjoy her retreat. He would have liked nothing more than to chase her, to hunt.

She shook her head, trying to clear whatever sensations were stealing over her, unsure how they could feel so much like her own. His mouth tweaked into something of pleasure, the firelight catching his dark eyes, a sickeningly familiar shade of blue. *Like sapphires*.

"Rhen." Nim stepped back, queasy at the name that had rolled off her tongue. She'd never said it before, had not felt it enter her mind, and yet, she knew. It was Calum's brother.

"Ahh," he murmured, stepping further into the light. "What a pleasure it is to finally meet you, Miss Weston." His voice was a satisfied purr that made Nim want to rip off her skin. Whatever Calum was, this man was worse.

He smiled as he sauntered closer then raised an elegant hand to playfully tap a fingertip to the end of his nose. "I see my suppositions have been wrong. You are not at all what I expected." His words said she was a stranger, but his intimations teased her with images, with the knowledge that an agent of the Trust had watched her sleep. He closed the distance, Nim's feet frozen to the ground, no part of her able to move, then took a half turn around her in his perusal before he came back to face her again. He hummed, the sound rumbling through Nim in a way that made her tremble with the urge to run. His face was so much like Calum's but younger, maybe five and twenty, and more mischievous, as if their meeting was a lark, some good-natured prank instead of his kidnapping of a citizen of Inara to drag into the depths of the undercity.

He chuckled, his teeth flashing in a malevolent grin, and Nim had the sensation he could tell what she was thinking, though she'd not spoken a word. She had to get away. She'd never been surer of anything in her life.

"My brothers have made a plaything out of you," Rhen said. "But you are no mouse, are you?" He reached forward to tap the end of Nim's nose as he'd done to his own and murmured, "No, I think not."

At her flinch, his smile fell into something more playful, catlike, and he slipped his hands behind his back in a gesture of casual ease. He *tsked* in disappointment, the sensation rolling off him. "Do not disappoint me, Miss Weston. You hold your tongue as if you were not the clever girl who played in their little game, who captured a prize of her own." He leaned forward, brow shifting conspiratorially, his intimation slithering over her skin. *Show me what you're made of.*

Nim fell to her knees before him, as if the power of his intimation was overwhelming. He couldn't know she'd downed Allister's tonic. She had a moment, a chance. That was all. She could feel Rhen standing before her, staring down as she doubled over, one hand pressed to her gut. The other, trembling and sweat-slicked, found the sheath beneath her skirt.

He wanted to see what she was made of. She wasn't sure she'd ever known. Once, she might have said she was like any other girl, a child of sweets and laughs and the bond she'd felt with her father... but at the idea, Nim's head snapped to the side. She gazed at the shadows beyond a low cell door, and her heart went cold. It was suddenly clear what lay beyond it. She'd not been dragged down to the cells to be thrown into one.

She was being shown where they had left her father and would be forced to witness what had become of him—if he remained there at all. She felt nothing from the darkness, no sense of the man he'd ever been. But she wouldn't have, as he had not been a man of magic. Her father had been only flesh and blood. He had been taken from her, stolen, and even the memory of him was a dangerous, deadly thing. Coldness swept through her, and had she to answer at that moment, Nim would have known precisely what she was made of. Not the innocence of a child but the cold, hard makings of a weapon.

She rose in one fluid motion, flesh and blood and vengeance come to life. The magic in the dagger or the steel in her resolve had broken whatever hold Calum's brother had over her, and the blade slammed into his gut, fast and deep, surely too easily for any strike that would cause real damage. But her aim had struck true, and Rhen's blood flowed over her hand. Her eyes met his, her resolve falling away at the sight of him, so young, so shocked, grievously wounded by her hand.

And then a cold fear swam through her as his shock melted, his mouth opening with his broken laugh. Nim had done something bad. She had to get away. Her hand seemed frozen on the dagger, her grip coated in blood, her fingers unwilling to release the weapon. Rhen leaned nearer and, through his cat's smile, whispered her name as if satisfied, sated, triumphant.

Nim jerked the dagger free and ran.

CHAPTER 10

Nim burst from the gateway and into Inara, disoriented by darkness. It had been barely afternoon when she was dragged beneath the city. Fates knew what awaited her or if she'd been knocked out longer than she'd thought, but nothing could slow her steps. Rhen was behind her, giving chase. She was his prey, and her pulse thrummed like a rabbit's.

His blood felt sticky on her hands, damning her. Rhen was an heir to the Trust. Rhen was Calum's brother.

Rhen is coming.

Nim would have been a fool to glance over her shoulder, but the fear that drove her was all she could obey. She turned, catching sight of a form moving through the catacombs she'd left behind, past the guards who had let her run, who had known she was his to track, and slammed into a solid body. She shrieked, jerking the dagger back to strike, and her wrist was caught in the iron grip of a large, male hand.

Warmth spread through her, a roiling, steady rage, and the dagger became something other than the magical bond it had been. The grip she'd been unable to release finally loosened, the weapon clattered to the stone, and Nim's body was wracked with a violent tremor. *Warrick*. Warrick had come. He held her against him, which was fortunate because she wasn't certain her legs were attached any longer, let alone in working order.

Nim took in the men at Warrick's back. Castle guard. Wesley. The king's men filling the street. She had never seen a king's man inside the Trust, and surely, given Warrick's deal, they were not allowed while under his command. She might have wondered how long the men had stood at the entrance to the Trust, how long she had been gone, but the heavy air and shifting shadows drew her notice. It had not turned to evening. The sky had gone dark as if a storm approached. Nim glanced at Warrick then followed his gaze to the arch that led to the undercity. Beneath the iron bars of the gateway, raised to evening revelers, Calum's brother shifted to stand in the torchlight.

Rhen, her mind seemed to whisper on repeat. Not just Calum's brother but Warrick's as well. Another danger. Another secret. He stood smiling, his jacket open to reveal a shirt soaked with blood drawn by Nim's hand. The stain spread like ink from his middle, seeping down the material on one side of his dark trousers. "Brother," Rhen said.

Warrick flinched, and though Nim could feel it beneath her touch, she could not take her eyes off Rhen to discover the reaction of the king's guard. *Brother*, he had said. It was a treacherous threat, one that had the potential to break the foundations of the kingdom. A cold emotion had settled deep within Warrick, but all Nim could focus on was the heat of his magic. He wanted retribution, wanted to burn. This brother was worse than Calum. This brother had done something wrong.

He has no care for our rules. Rhen's intimation seemed to mock, as if he were speaking as Warrick. But Warrick said nothing, only looked on.

Rhen slid a hand to his hip and wagged his eyebrows, impish and gamesome, as if he'd not just been stabbed. He leaned forward, his intimation plain: *Come get me.*

Warrick shifted, and Nim thought for a heartbeat that he

would, but he had made a bargain that had not been broken, one that kept Inara safe in trade and said that Warrick could not walk into the Trust. He leaned over, picked up the bloodied dagger, and shoved it into his belt. His gaze met Nim's for only a moment, then he tugged her to him and turned to walk away from the Trust.

WARRICK DID NOT SPEAK on their return to the castle but only held her against him atop a large black horse as the sky roiled before its storm then carried her inside as if her legs would not take her. She could not say for certain that they would have, though the trembling had stopped, but his grip on her seemed to be more of a dare that anyone try to touch her. He took her to his rooms, leaving a crestfallen and weary Wesley in the sitting room, where Wes gave Nim a miserable look steeped in apology before sliding into a chair. Warrick continued to his study, stood Nim before the desk, and handed her a drink. He produced a basin, and as Nim washed the blood from her hands, she had to look away from the water, tinted and sloshing and wanting anything left in her to rise again.

She closed her eyes, and Warrick ran a damp cloth over her face then unfastened her ruined dress. It dropped to the floor, and she stepped out of it along with her ruined slippers. Warrick tossed his jacket over a chair before laying the dagger on the desk beside her. Nim stared down at it. She had stabbed both of Warrick's brothers now, drawn blood from the heirs to the Trust.

Without a word, Warrick slid his hands beneath Nim's back and knees and lifted her to carry into his room. *Their room*, he seemed to think, but Warrick was wrong. She'd fouled up their plans. They hadn't met for their ceremony, hadn't followed through with his intentions. Rhen had called him "brother" in front of the castle guard.

So much was wrong, but when Warrick settled Nim onto the

bed and lay beside her to wrap his arm over her and draw her near, all she could do was sigh in relief. Fates save her, but she could not believe she'd made it out alive. No part of her had thought she would escape the depths of the undercity, even as she'd stabbed the man who held her there. She had broken their law by harming Rhen. The accountants had broken Inara law on his order by stealing her. "Hush," Warrick whispered, though Nim had not spoken a word. He ran a finger gently over her temple then smoothed the hair back from her face. *Hush*, he thought in a calming tone. *Hush*, as if to quiet both their fears.

Nim breathed in his scent and let the warmth of his body seep through her shift as the warmth of his magic settled into her bones. She belonged there with him. It wasn't only Warrick's presence that called to her in a way that felt safe, felt like home. It was his magic. But as she lay there, she could not even recall the part of her that had always feared Calum's power, that had recoiled from the feel of it and the mere idea of it touching her in any form. She drew in another long breath then opened her eyes to the dimly lit room. She'd been trying to escape the magic that wanted her. She had run from it since she was a girl. And now, nothing felt righter than leaping into its arms.

"You have a new wardrobe and a vanity table." Her voice was hoarse and felt disused. It came to her that she hadn't spoken to Rhen aside from that single word, the name he'd forced from her lips before she'd sealed them shut. For some reason, the idea of depriving him his game felt nearly as pleasant as having stabbed him. It was certainly less messy.

Warrick seemed caught off guard by her announcement, drawing his face from where it had pressed into her hair to follow her gaze. Across the room, opposite his chest of drawers, was a tall wardrobe beside a small table and mirror. "Yes."

It was all he said, but she sensed a flash of intimation, that he had brought it there for her. It was *their* room, and in it, *her* things. "I've mucked up your plans again," she said.

He settled his head onto the pillow once more and made the noncommittal sound she liked so much.

"What now?"

His fingers toyed idly with the material of her shift. "We carry on as planned. I'll make new arrangements with the magistrate, and we'll have it done." An undercurrent of wrath flowed beneath his words, promising that Rhen would never touch her again.

"We need to complete the ceremony so that he cannot reach me?"

Warrick did not answer, but she felt from him that the entire ordeal was more complicated than that.

She turned to face him, her bare toes brushing against his booted shin. "But you can't tell me things." Things like the fact that Calum and Rhen were his brothers. Things about magic.

He reached to brush a thumb over her cheek, to offer her comfort and promises she could sense before he'd even spoken them, but the neck of his shirt shifted. At Nim's horrified expression, Warrick froze.

Her gaze found his, no sign of the matter or that he'd kept it from her in his eyes. But she could feel the truth hiding beneath his intimations. She sat up, pressing him to his back as she leaned over him, over the new wounds that marked his chest and shoulder. There was nothing but resignation in his response, not a single regret for what he'd done. She pulled the material of his shirt aside to see it all, her stomach dropping at the truth of what he'd done.

"The dagger?" she whispered, her fingers tracing lightly over the fresh scars that feathered into the old. They would hurt him for as long as he lived, a reminder of what he'd done, what the magic had cost him.

Warrick did not answer. But she could see the accusation was right. He had tied himself to her, woven his magic into the blade, and when she'd struck true it not only tore a sacrifice from Warrick but failed to release Nim until she'd slammed into him outside the Trust. Returned to him. He had paid for what she had done to Rhen with his own flesh.

"Is this what happens," she said, her eyes meeting his in the small space between them, "when magic is given freely?" Some sort of debt, she meant, a sacrifice that was paid and an act put into motion that would not be satisfied until it reached its end—until she had come back to him, until the magic in the dagger had let go its hold.

Warrick's hand rose to cover hers over his chest. She could feel his heartbeat beneath her palm, strong and steady. He was not afraid. He could not be sorry for what he'd done. He would not let Rhen touch her again.

"No matter what it costs you?" Her words were harsher than she'd intended, too loud in the sparsely decorated room.

He opened his mouth to speak, but the vow she expected, his heated reply, was cut short. He frowned. "One moment, Wesley." Nim had not even heard the boy, but Warrick was moving off the bed and crossing the room in haste to grab a gown from the new wardrobe. Her wardrobe. He laid the fine dark silk on the bed and gave her a long look before turning to walk from the room.

Nim was not certain what the look promised, but she did know that she had to get dressed. Someone was coming. Warrick had been summoned. She stared at the dress for a moment then crossed to the wardrobe to open its doors. New dresses waited inside, nothing familiar to those in her own room.

The king had certainly heard about their confrontation. The king would know Nim had been dragged to the Trust and that his seneschal had nearly followed her inside, at risk to the kingdom.

The king had promised to end her.

Face twisting, Nim shoved the dresses aside and jerked from its hook the wardrobe of her new post as constable.

CHAPTER 11

Nim burst from Warrick's room dressed in trousers and a slim jacket, the light cape attached at her shoulders trailing behind her. She did not find Warrick or the king waiting, only Wesley, posted at the door to the sitting room, wearing an uneasy expression. Nim blinked at him, and he gave her a cringing, apologetic sort of smile. She crossed the room to stand in front of him then crossed her arms.

"Warrick says I'm to bar you from leaving this room."

She raised an eyebrow.

"I'm going to do it, Nim. He's been summoned by the king."

Nim dropped her arms. "Wes, I appreciate your loyalty, but I'm afraid I'm not about to go along with it. No part of me is willing to stand here and wait to be gathered by the king's guards." Wesley's forehead wrinkled. Nim glanced over her shoulder then moved to Warrick's desk. The dagger still lay there, covered in Rhen's blood. She dipped it into the basin then shook the water free and wiped the blade on her cloak. When she strapped it to the sheath at her thigh, Wes moved forward.

"Nim, this is a very bad idea."

She glanced up at him. "Do you know what the king intends to do?" His expression made it clear that he had no idea. "End me," she said. "The moment he discovers I'm tied to the Trust, this is over. All of it. And nothing Warrick can do will save me." In fact, she suspected that would suit the Trust just fine. A rift would form between the king and his heir, and Calum and his lot would be that much closer to their prize.

"You can't believe—"

"He told me," Nim snapped. "In just as plain terms." She straightened, grabbed a taper, then crossed to the tinderbox. When she turned again, Wes was there.

"I can't let you leave. He's only trying to keep you safe."

She sighed. "I'm sorry to make you break your word. Truly, I am. But Wes, what will Warrick do should you not do as he's asked?"

"He'll be disappointed."

"And?"

His reply was soft. "And I don't like to disappoint him."

"Neither do I," Nim said. "But I'd rather not be hanged by the king."

Wesley's lips pursed. "Where are you going?"

"To find out about magic."

His gaze narrowed.

"The dungeon."

"Nim." He strung the word out, and his shoulders sagged in a way that made him appear younger.

"It's the only way out of this, Wes. You know who I am. You know what they've done to me. If I don't find a way around it, I'm doomed to repeat the same situations as happened today." Worse, even. She firmed her resolve. "I'll not let them use me to take down the kingdom."

He let out a long-suffering huff. "Then I'm coming with you."

She started to tell him no, that he didn't have to, but she understood who Wes was. More, she knew what protection he could offer against magic. She gave him a sharp nod and turned to the hidden panel that led to the corridor.

In the darkness, Nim remembered the sensation of being followed the night before and paused, letting that part of her reach out and try to find the sense that had clued her in to magic in the past. She felt nothing but the fidgeting of Wesley behind her, breaking his vow to the person he respected most, his unease patent even in the dark. She frowned but pushed forward, turning down the corridor that led past her suite of rooms.

Wes tugged her cape. She glanced back, the taper throwing flickering shadows at odd angles through the narrow space and catching on Wes's mop of red hair. "This way is shorter," he whispered, gesturing toward a corridor that branched off the one she knew.

She handed Wes the light, allowing him to lead the way. They followed the path through more turns and down a spiral of stairs and eventually came out into a room adjacent to the corridor that led to Calum's cell. It explained how Warrick had so quickly found her the first night she'd come down.

"Ready?" Wesley whispered.

Not at all. She set her jaw and nodded.

In the corridor, the guards came to attention, though it was plain they'd heard something before the new royal constable and the seneschal's messenger came into view. Nim and Wesley strode forward as if doing so was part of those duties and not some ill-advised lark they would likely pay for later. She could only hope it was later, anyway.

They stopped before the lot of guards, three visible and surely a few others in the shadowed corners nearby. The front guard eyed them both. Fates what they were, the nearest guard turned out to be the same one Nim had threatened with a magic sword.

Wesley winced then inclined his head toward the man. "Bramwell, pleasure to see you again."

He grunted. It was not the pleasant, noncommittal sort.

"We need through." Nim's voice wasn't as commanding as she

might have wanted. She was going to have to practice wielding authority. "By order of the seneschal."

She felt Wes flinch beside her, but he managed to hold back any other reaction.

Bramwell crossed his arms. "Is that so?"

The other guards exchanged a laughing glance, the look at odds with their stern mouths and solemn postures. Nim gave Bramwell a steady stare. "Are you asking me to repeat myself?"

His arms dropped, shoulders stiffening. "We receive our 'orders from the seneschal' directly from the seneschal. Anyone who was truly coming on his word would know that, *my lady*."

"He's in with the king on urgent business," Wesley said. "Surely, you've heard." It was not a lie, though Nim wondered whether misleading Warrick's men would cost Wes or the guard in the end.

The guard's gaze narrowed. "I expect the pair of you are going to find yourselves on the unpleasant end of an interroga-tion." At Nim's expression, he shook his head. "But the seneschal, as you say, has left a standing order to allow you through—should you ever request it—as long as he or his messenger are present at the time."

Nim felt her gaze slide to Wes, who appeared equally sheep-ish. "Excellent," she managed, though she felt especially small, given that Warrick had shown her trust while her own deceit was surely about to be reported on by his guard. "Do go on."

He gave her a look but turned to unlatch the lock.

The guard did not follow to Calum's cell, but the door did not close behind them. Wes held onto Nim's cape more, she thought, for the protection against magic he could offer than that he was cowed by Calum's presence. When they stopped before the cell bars, Nim was glad Wes had come, that Wes could see—like she had—that the danger was contained.

A chuckle echoed through the darkness, the torches unlit since Warrick was not there to fire them with his magic. She held the taper forward, casting light toward the alcove that made up Calum's cell. "Back so soon?" he purred, his intimation making clear that he was not surprised, while his teasing tone suggested that she could not bear to be without him.

Nim thought his cell might have been better suited if it was the size of the one her father had been shoved into. "I've stabbed your brother."

She had a moment's satisfaction at the shock Calum let slip before he stepped forward. "Already? They do say marriage wilts the bloom off its rose, but I daresay that's impressive, my lady, even for you."

She took a small step toward the bars. "Not him. The other."

Calum's eyes glinted dangerously in the light, his intimation a spear of emotion Nim couldn't sort. "Come to gloat, Miss Weston? A bit unsporting of you while I'm caged."

"He captured me on the street."

Calum did not seem to react to her words, but she couldn't gauge whether the lack of concern was due to Rhen's temperament not making such an act surprising or that Calum wasn't at all worried about his brother breaking the rules.

Or maybe, she worried, Rhen wasn't bound to the same rules at all. That was what she needed, to understand their rules, had she any chance to survive the game they played. She leaned forward, letting the light reveal both their faces. "He took me to my father's cell. You are familiar with the one, I'm sure, as you shoved him in there while I was only a girl."

The ease in Calum's expression was clearly forced. Nim straightened. "I'm thinking of redecorating your cell, as a matter of fact. Feeling quite inspired after my experience."

"Something with a low ceiling." The voice from beside her was startling, so low and level that it did not sound like Wesley at first.

"Yes," Nim agreed. "Dark and small." Like Calum's heart.

Calum chuckled, pressing a palm to his chest over an unreasonably tidy vest and shirt. "You wound me, dove. And here, I thought we'd come to an agreement."

There was the thing she had wanted to forget. Nim could do nothing to Calum that would break their contract, despite the magical dagger strapped to her thigh. She would only ever have what he gave her and what she managed to steal. Calum would never freely aid her, and his intimations were too full of lies to be much use. She was wasting her time with him. She needed to find another way. *Dove*, he had called her, one more taunt while he was behind bars. She flicked a finger against the metal, letting the sound be the last word, but as she turned to go, with Wes giving Calum a final cold look, the intimation that came was only for her.

You think I'm the one in a cage, little bird, but it's been you all along.

CHAPTER 12

Nim and Wes stole back through the corridors to the upper hallways and the study designated for Nim's new post as constable. Two guards waited outside the doorway, and Nim nearly turned to head another way, but her gaze caught on a familiar figure seated in the corridor just beyond the guards. "Margery."

Wes's gaze shot up to find her, as if only realizing Nim had fallen back upon hearing her whispered word. His posture straightened, and they strode forward together to meet the guard.

Margery stood, an elegant hand smoothing the material of her skirt. She gave Nim's wardrobe a once-over, entirely ignoring the two men in king's colors whom, if Nim had had to guess, she'd been giving a difficult time. "Lady Weston," she said, her tone short and sharply refined.

Nim inclined her head. "Lady Margery."

Margery's gaze flicked to Wes, who took her cue expertly and marched right past the guards who had apparently barred her from entering. Her chin rose as she strode past them and into the room ahead of Nim, then Wes shut the door behind the three of them.

When they reached her desk, Nim turned. "Margery—"

Her friend held up a hand. "No need for explanations. Half of Inara is afire with chatter about the Trust kidnapping an agent of the king." Nim winced, but Margery only leaned forward, gesturing between Nim and Wes. "You two look like you're up to some trouble. While I cannot say I'm not wounded that you didn't request my assistance, and though I do find it quite agreeable that every time you're attacked in broad daylight and miss one of our meetings the seneschal of our great Inara takes the time to send a personal message that you are safe and well, I'm done waiting. I am here to aid you, whether you've asked for it or not."

Nimona opened her mouth to argue that getting tangled in Trust business was not something she intended to let her friend participate in, but Margery cut her short with a level glare. She was grateful in such moments that Margery did not have the ability to send intimations.

Margery's gaze snapped to Wes to give him a similar warning glare, but the boy only grinned. She nodded as if the matter was sorted and settled into a chair beside the desk. "Now, what are we working on?"

Nim crumpled into her own chair with a sigh, and Wes said, "I'll send some tea and check on..." His words fell off before he could add either "Warrick" or "the king," and Nim hoped the boy wasn't in too much trouble for letting her escape.

When he closed the door behind him, Margery trained her dark eyes on Nim. "Trouble in paradise?"

"The king wants me dead."

Margery gave Nim an assessing look. "I can see that."

She shook her head. "He warned me, plainly, that should I give him one excuse—" She made a slicing gesture at her neck.

Margery hummed. "Being publicly snatched from the street and dragged to the Trust is a fairly solid excuse, then."

Nim nodded.

"So how do we fix it?"

Nim shrugged and gestured to the pile of documents on her desk. "I'm afraid my only recourse is to make it as difficult for him as possible. As for the rest, I'm hoping to learn what I can to figure out how the bindings work and what I can do to subvert magic's hold on me."

Leaning forward, Margery asked, "What hold? Warrick broke your contract, and we wrote a new one to bind Calum. What is left to hold you?"

"I-I don't like to talk about it."

Margery reached forward and patted her hand. "I understand. I wouldn't dare be petty enough to remind you that your secret keeping is precisely why we had trouble the last time, but know that whatever it is, you have my support."

Nim pursed her lips. "I don't know exactly how or why, but magic calls to me, draws me to it." She did not mention the head of the Trust, the dark queen whose magic had called to her, strongest of all, nor that the queen's youngest son had not merely kidnapped Nim but had been inside her very rooms.

"And this is the bond you want to break?"

Thoughts of Warrick's magic, warm and safe, swam through her. "I don't... well, I'm not sure that it's the call of magic that is the trouble, only that I'm afraid of the connection it has made to someone specific." Someone other than Warrick.

Margery's expression fell for a brief moment before she shook herself and squeezed Nim's hand. "Right. So we'll sort this out." She looked at the papers on Nim's desk. "What's all this, then? Where do we start?"

HOURS PASSED in the candlelit study, the sky cloudy and dark through the windows outside. The remainder of the tea Wes had sent up had long since grown cold, and Nim was exhausted, having been both kidnapped and certain she'd be hanged in a single day. Her thoughts kept returning to Rhen, how he'd so easily slipped into her mind, and how he'd been near so many times when she'd sensed only the barest of magic.

"I can keep searching," Margery said without looking up from her task. "You go ahead and snatch whatever sleep you can."

"I'm perfectly fine." Nim's declaration was broken by a yawn that would not be contained, but when Margery glanced up, her expression was not the expected smirk. Suddenly alert, Nim straightened. "What is it?"

Margery slid the parchment across the desk and tapped a signature. "Avery Preston." Nim glanced up from the paper, unfamiliar with the name. "Lord Preston was party to an agreement I wrote up for a king's advisor. The terms were strangely specific, given that in the final revisions, it was asked that Preston's name be stricken from every single page. And then the dolt who'd asked for him to be included in the first place had the gall to suggest I forget he'd ever said it. I do not forget," Margery said. "Particularly when suggestions border the line of threats." She leaned back, one of her dark brows shifting into a knowing spike. "I looked into it a bit afterward, as one does. He's cousin to an old Darby line."

The Darbys were a distant offshoot to the king. It was a reach, yes, but Stewart's potential heirs would have been no one close. The king's family had been taken by accident and illness when he was a young man.

Nim read through the document, and all of it seemed innocuous. It had likely only made it to her desk because it had been collected with other scraps and scrolls taken from someone the guard had been looking into. "I'm not sure," Nim murmured, but something drew her fingers to slide over the name. A quiet gasp echoed through the room as she snatched them back.

"What was that?" Margery asked.

"The sting of magic." Nim's gaze roamed the document again. She drew a needed breath. "I'll request an inquiry into him and, I don't know, call him in for questioning?"

Margery's mouth settled into a line as she considered. "Is that the best tactic? To face him so boldly? He's not exactly of low standing. What if we instead call on those around him? Not close enough to draw his concern, only so that we are better positioned to discover his activities and associates."

Nim felt her heart swell at her friend's liberal use of "we." She would rather that Margery was safely tucked away in her family's manor. Even with what the Trust had done to Margery's father aside, she was crossing a dangerous line just by offering aid. Nim opened her mouth to thank her again, but the lock on the study door clicked, and both women turned to regard the opening door.

Maris stepped in, giving a practiced curtsy before meeting Nim's gaze. "My lady, I've been sent to fetch you back to your rooms. Will you be taking dinner with your guest?"

"Yes," Margery said. "I'll be staying all evening."

Maris's attention never faltered, her dark eyes steady on Nim. Nim nodded and stood, and Maris dipped again before turning toward the door. As Margery stood to follow, she shot Nim a look conveying that she was highly impressed. "What?" Nim mouthed.

Margery tipped her head toward Maris at the door and whispered, "You rated a queen's protector?"

Glancing sidelong at Maris's waiting back, Nim mouthed, "She's a lady's maid."

Margery smirked and strode forward past a gaping Nim to follow Maris from the study. When they reached Nim's suite and Maris left to fetch their dinner, Margery pursed her lips in a silent whistle, leisurely examining the room. "Someone holds you in high regard. You do have him hooked, don't you?" she murmured with a chuckle.

Nim crossed to her writing desk to scratch out a quick message. As Margery examined a vase and sculpture atop the mantel, Nim returned the quill to its spot and dusted the ink. By the time Maris returned with their dinner, Nim had the request for inquiry into Lord Preston folded, sealed, and ready to be delivered via Wesley. Wes would have informed Warrick that Margery was with Nim, and she was fairly certain that was the only reason the seneschal had not tracked her down as soon as he'd discovered she'd escaped his rooms. Maris or Wesley would also have reported that Margery intended to stay the night. She forced her gaze away from the wall that hid the secret corridor to Warrick's room.

"Keep worrying your lip like that, and you're likely to make it bleed."

Nim gave Margery a look, but she only shrugged and gestured at the table. "You've been sent a feast. Might as well enjoy."

"Because I could be hanged by morning?"

Margery frowned. "Well, yes, not the most preferable. But fates take it all, I suppose that it might be our last is as good a reason as any to relish a meal."

Running a hand over her face, Nim flopped onto the settee beside the table. "No, Margery, I'll not let you share in this. If I'm to be hanged, I insist I go it alone."

"Come now," Margery said. "A good biscuit can solve anything. We'll sort it out. Fill your stomach." She handed Nim a plate and settled beside her with a dish of her own. "I have to say it, love. Aside from being an enemy of the king, your situation here is quite agreeable. You've been given the best accommodations and staff, you're allowed free rein to follow your interests, and the work suits you, always engaging with just enough potential for risk. And I suspect it satisfies your penchant for cracking down on poor morals."

Nim snorted. "Who am I to judge morals? I'm a criminal. Enemy to the kingdom."

"Only on paper, dear."

"Paper is what matters."

Margery's lips tweaked into a smile as she eyed her plate. "You would think so, wouldn't you?" Her tone was light, but underneath, Nim felt the reminder that paper could be torn up. Contracts could be rewritten.

CHAPTER 13

Nim did not recall having fallen asleep but awoke in her bed, her hair unbound and boots removed, the blankets a tangle around her bare legs. She blinked, narrowing her bleary eyes across the room to where Margery and Maris were seated in the sunlight streaming through the window, deep in low-spoken conversation and surrounded by plates of half-eaten cake. Nim groaned.

"Oh good," Margery called over her shoulder. "You've awakened before midday."

Nim sat up in time to see Maris tighten her lips in a suppressed smile. "What are you two about?"

Margery waved a dismissive hand over her shoulder. "Planning, dear. It's all resolved. Have a bath and a bite to eat, and we'll be dressed in time for a stroll through the garden before you're due."

She set her bare feet on the cool wood floor. "Due for what?"

Maris's shoulders straightened. "A royal gathering, my lady."

Nim's head fell back to stare at the canopy above her bed. "Must we?"

"Yes," the two women said in unison.

And so it was that by late afternoon, Nim's person had been

powdered, perfumed, and coiffed into a state beyond any it had ever experienced. Margery had stood across the room, taking her in with a narrowed eye then giving her nod of approval before she became distracted by her own preparations. As Nim waited for their departure, Maris fiddled with the beads at Nim's neck, her dark eyes skirting the disconcertingly low split on the front of the gown.

"Maris," Nim whispered, "I was told you were a lady's maid."

Maris's expression did not change, and her gaze never moved from her work. "Aye, my lady."

There was something final in the lie, a tone that intended to close the conversation. Nim snatched the quill from the table beside them then drove it fast and hard toward Maris, whose wrist moved with such force that the quill flew out of Nim's hand to clatter onto the floor across the room. Margery snorted a laugh.

Maris gave Nim a level look, her mouth turned down in something that might have been disappointment and might have been annoyance at the test.

"You planned to bring me tea and braid my hair to eternity and never mention this?"

Maris straightened. "I did. And I do."

Nim crossed her arms.

"My duty is to protect and provide, my lady, by order of the seneschal. I can protect you no better than while I am near, and I am serving the kingdom should that duty call for me to pour your tea or use my sword."

Nim let her gaze rake over the maid, swordless as she was.

Maris rolled her eyes. "I would be remiss in my duty if I allowed everyone to see that I was a threat. Would you not agree?"

"So you hid it from me because I'm a threat?"

Margery let go another pointed sound of amusement, and Nim snapped her mouth shut. There was a press to Maris's lips that said well enough that no one was more a threat to Nim than herself. "Very well," she said. "But no more secrets."

Maris's lips twitched, implying that she was aware Nim had a few more secrets than her maid, but she only curtsied before she backed away. "Aye, my lady. Now you know my secret. Let us hope you never again need it."

The word "again" drew Nim up short, sticking any retort well and truly inside her throat. Thoughts of Rhen and the sapphires rose anew.

Margery dropped her brush to the vanity table and stood, apparently unaware of the shift in Nim's mood. "Now, then, let's off to disinter the camarilla."

THE BANQUET HALL was filled with dozens of courtiers and kingdom officials but done up with little pomp or celebration. Gatherings were nothing like the balls and festivals held by the king, events Nim had rarely seen in person, but instead less formal and more widely attended meetings of those who decided how Inara was run and those like herself, she realized with a start, responsible for carrying out the king's rule. Her palms went slick with apprehension, but Margery tucked her arm easily into the crook of one of Nim's to lead them through the room.

In a slim silk gown, Margery was in her element, throwing mocking smiles and pointed comments at the worst of the court, not slowing to wait for their response. She was like a cat, above reproach and uninterested in anyone who promised interest in her. Margery loathed the sycophants who spent their days vying for the king's ear so they might use his power against those beneath them. And as someone responsible for their private contracts and deeds, Margery knew well enough precisely who misused their posts and abused the king's favor. Such had happened far more frequently in recent years, since Nim's father and the king's other trusted advisors had disappeared. Stewart had few he could trust.

Nim's eyes cut across the crowd, and she amended that maybe he had none at all.

The pair of them traversed the long hall toward those of higher standing, toward the dais, where the king's table sat empty with sunlight streaming in from the tall windows and streaking across the bedecked forms of lords and ladies awaiting his arrival. Beyond the dais was a monstrous tapestry that spanned nearly the entire back wall, its scenes depicting a succession of historic events in Inara's past—any act of King Stewart not among them.

Fingers hovering lightly over where the material of her own gown hid the magical dagger strapped to her thigh, Nim let her gaze trail over the esteemed and influential of Inara. She did not recognize the faces from her childhood, though many held familiar expressions of scorn. She wondered who among them remembered her as Bancroft Weston's daughter and how many only saw her as a new threat to the positions they held so dear.

"Lady Margery."

The smooth voice snapped Nim's attention back to her immediate surroundings, where Margery had been approached by two elderly women in the formal robes of the treasury, one silver-haired with age, the other's dark braids only streaked with gray. "Nim," Margery said with not a single hint of insincerity, "it is my great pleasure to introduce you to two of the best sort: Lady Constance, Master of Coin, and her assistant, Lady Lora. Ladies, this is your new constable, Lady Nimona Weston."

Lady Constance's gaze was sharp, her smile slow. She surely remembered Nim's father and that he was of the best sort too. "It is my honor," Lady Constance said, "and far past time we saw new blood in the constable's office. Our dear seneschal is quite particular about who he takes in."

Margery didn't appear even to attempt to mask the wicked-ness in the grin she gave Nim. "Oh, indeed," she said. "I've never met a man whose trust was rarer. But you'll find the lady Nimona quite up to the task."

"How do you like it?" Lady Constance asked, the lines around pale eyes not tarnishing what was still a striking face.

"Very well," Nim said. "Though to be truthful, I've barely settled into the role."

"Do tell us stories of the seneschal," Margery cut in. "Some delightful gossip she might lord over him, should the position become too tedious."

Constance made a sound that was nearly a snort but managed to cover it with a thin cough. The quirk in her lip shifted into something more reflective. "Aye, but I have known him since he was a stripling, haven't I? He was a quiet boy, watchful and well-mannered. Loyal to the kingdom. I don't find he's changed a great deal since then." Her appraising gaze raked over Nim. "I do wonder what goes on in that head of his sometimes. If the seneschal has a flaw, it's that he's too private. And if you ask me, a man who strives to keep his personal affairs close to the vest in a crowd like this... well, that's no sort of flaw at all."

"Unless his business is collecting corpses in the closet," Lady Lora added with a laugh.

The three women glanced at her while Lady Constance cleared her throat. "Ah, speak of a desire, and the fates shall deliver it."

Margery's grin broke wide as she turned to follow the older woman's gaze. Across the hall, the crowd bowed and parted, making way for the man who was second to the king. Behind him, a wave of lords and ladies followed, though Nim knew from her research when he'd been merely her next mark that Warrick was not the sort one could approach easily to gain favor or to catch his ear. It did not make him less a target, apparently. All eyes were on him, or she might have heeded the instinct to turn away before she was caught looking. Warrick was every bit the venerable seneschal his reputation had promised. He was regal in the robes of his office, a slim shirt and dark vest beneath, his sword at his hip. The coronet nestled into his dark hair shone as brightly as his gaze, the latter of which skirted the crowd with practiced ease.

Fates save her, but she was a fool for the man.

Margery leaned closer to whisper, "Are you thinking what I am?"

"That I'm a fool?"

She laughed outright, and Warrick's gaze cut to both of them at the sound. Nim nudged her friend with an elbow as she straightened.

"Lord Warrick," Lady Constance said from behind them when he approached. Nim and Margery gave a small curtsy as they widened the circle.

Warrick inclined his head. "Lady Constance, I see you've been introduced to our new constable." He gave nods to each in the group. "Lady Lora, Lady Margery." Margery winked conspiratorially, and he rewarded her with a slight frown before his eyes met Nim's. There was only a heartbeat of hesitation, but in it came an intimation that felt like regret. He had not meant to introduce her as merely his constable. Nim had escaped from his rooms then been sequestered with Margery. She'd avoided him on purpose, and they both knew it. "My lady."

Nim dipped her chin. As she did, Warrick's intimation slipped further, and she felt something more. He hadn't merely been concerned that he'd wanted to cement their bond with the vows or that he'd wanted to present her as his wife before all the king's advisers and every officer of the kingdom. Warrick was worried that she'd avoided him for a far darker reason: she'd been disturbed that Rhen had called him "brother." She raised her eyes to meet his.

Warrick didn't know she'd already uncovered the secret. Indeed, he'd been raised to understand that if any secret was worse than a closet full of corpses, as Lady Lora had said, it was that he held magic in his blood.

He seemed to tighten his emotions and draw back any intimation but one: they would complete the ceremony tonight, before the king moved to have her questioned. If she would have him.

Heat rose in Nim's cheeks, but given their witnesses, she was unable to give any answer aside from a single, sharp nod. She forced her gaze back to Lady Constance, certain she could not hold any respectable expression with Margery examining the exchange. Margery murmured something to Warrick, but when Nim's gaze fell back onto the pair, Warrick's attention was on a man near the dais. "If you'll excuse me, ladies. I hate to leave good company, but—"

Margery laughed, a light and lovely sound that seemed entirely genuine. "Lord Warrick, do trust that women of our caliber recognize full well when the wolves have begun to circle."

The grim set to his mouth was a sort of agreement, but he only made farewells before he left the group. Nim tried not to watch him go, feeling slightly untethered and unsure where else she might look. The room did feel a bit like circling wolves were about, and she thought she might want to skin Maris and Margery for forcing her into a gown for show rather than the robes of her station, not that she would have had much chance in a scuffle with either of them, the viragoes.

There was a muffled commotion at the opposite end of the hall, the familiar shuffling of feet and turning of bodies as conversation fell to a hush in anticipation of the king. Nim turned with the rest, facing the dais and prepared to bow, thinking she must have broken into a sweat, given how she'd been hit with a sudden chill. She glanced at Margery, who faced forward, eyes alert but shoulders relaxed as if nothing was amiss.

King Stewart strode into the room, a heavy robe draped from one shoulder, his armor shining bare on the other. As the room dipped into their bows, Stewart took the throne, settling in with a heaviness that seemed to convey a bit of anger or some other emotion Nim could not decipher. Warrick bowed beside the men he'd been in conversation with then walked forward and onto the dais to stand beside Stewart, his gaze straight ahead but noticeably not focused on the crowd. Nim resisted the urge to glance behind her and search for whatever he might see.

Wes, another among Warrick's men whom the king was not particularly partial to but another Warrick meant to protect, was absent.

The king's large hand twitched on the arm of the chair, his massive gold ring knocking against the wood. The room fell still and silent. He let them wait before he finally spoke.

"The great kingdom of Inara, bestowed upon our forefathers by the fates in time before record and treasured by its citizens in all the moons since, has withstood battles far beyond our ken. By their crowns and their blood, the kings before me have vowed to protect her and all she calls her own."

A murmur of approval rose through the crowd, but Nim only felt the chill slide further down her back. Stewart's deep voice echoed through the hall with a strange sort of finality that she could not quite pin down, as if some decision had been made, some choice resolved. His gaze roamed over the crowd. "Each in attendance here has also sworn a vow, given their oath to serve the kingdom and to uphold the laws laid in place ages before our time, laws that secure Inara's very foundation."

Nim's throat went thick as the sensation of phantom fingers slid across her neck. She swatted a hand against her skin before she could stop herself, and Warrick's gaze snapped to hers at the sound in the hushed hall.

Margery was glancing at her sidelong, but Nim did not allow herself to search the crowd. She found herself frozen by Stewart's next words: "One day ago, a representative of our great kingdom was accosted by a group of men known to trade in magical favors."

An intimation of shock came from Warrick, sharp and cold, but he averted his gaze as quickly as it had hit her. He could not let them see, could not give away that he'd searched her out in the crowd. Worse, Nim thought, that the king had not told Warrick what he had planned. Warrick was realizing what it meant, and he'd not removed Nim from the room and out of Stewart's reach. Her stomach swam.

"The assailants have been taken into custody, and though the incident remains under investigation, the four in hand who have trespassed on our land and have so blatantly disregarded the gravest law of all"—Stewart's green eyes cut to Nim in a reminder of the line he'd warned her not to cross—"will be hanged unto death before tomorrow's moon."

Nim's knees went weak. Stewart was still talking, but she could not focus on his words. Margery's hand slid into the crook of Nim's arm, but there was nothing gentle in the gesture. Bile rose in her throat, and she had to fight the urge to throw her friend's support off and run from the room. It was not the threat of being hanged like the men who had attacked her—it was that magic, dark and menacing, had slithered over her skin.

Someone was in the room... someone whose magic felt like Calum's and Rhen's.

CHAPTER 14

Nim forced herself to straighten, but before she could warn Margery they needed to go, Lady Lora fell to the floor. She hit with a solid smack, though her body was muffled by the material of her skirts. The landing had surely wounded her if the magic hadn't killed her outright. And it was magic, without question—Nim could feel it. Her eyes shot to the dais, and she knew Warrick could feel it, too, as he was already moving, hand on his sword, shoving through a crowd of lords and ladies who stared in shock.

Warrick shouldn't be coming. Warrick should stand by the king.

Margery had hold of Nim and tried to drag her from the commotion as Lady Constance and three others knelt over Lady Lora to discern the cause of her fall. As they rolled her over, a line of blood raced from her temple and onto the stone. Warrick reached them and stared at Nim, indecision flickering through his emotions. She should not have been his concern, even if she could sense it was all he was thinking of. "I'll find Wesley," she mouthed. Wesley could keep her safe from the magic.

Warrick's jaw went tight, but he gave a small nod. He was shouting orders before he'd even looked away, demanding guards to formation to protect the king and ordering that the castle entrances be barred.

Margery shoved Nim through the crowd and into the corridor with guards at their backs. They were rushed from the hall toward Warrick's rooms, but the sensation of magic lingered on Nim's skin, a crawling, prickling thing. The magic could have dropped her, the same as Lady Lora. Someone was toying with Nim. She tried to focus and remember what Rhen said to her alone beneath Inara and what Calum had said in his cell.

She had broken her contract with Calum. But she had not broken her bonds to the Trust. The magic still called to her, wanting her to turn, to go back to the hall, to the dark magic and to Warrick. She would have to be a fool to put herself within reach of the magic in the king's presence. Nothing could be done to save her from the king if her secret was revealed with so many witnesses. Whether Warrick meant to protect her or not, Inara would not stand for her connection to the magic—regardless that it had been done *to* her and not by her choice at all. Magic was a danger. The king was a danger.

Both of them wanted her.

Something like a laugh echoed through her senses, and Nim's steps faltered, the intimation she'd felt suddenly clear. *I'll see you soon*, it said. *So very soon.*

Margery's hand on her arm snapped Nim's attention back to the corridor. Nim glanced over her shoulder. "We need to get to Wesley."

Five guards followed them in and scattered about Warrick's sitting room among Nim, Margery, and Wes.

"What happened?" Wes asked.

Margery pursed her lips. "Though I do treasure the boy, why did we just run to Wesley?"

Nim gave the guards a glance. "Please wait outside."

"We have orders, my lady. You are not to be left alone."

She frowned. "I have Wesley."

The look the guard returned seemed to beg her not to make him disparage the boy's fighting skills right in front of him.

"Very well," Nim said. "Send in Maris."

He opened his mouth to reply then pressed it into a hard line as he gave a quick nod to the beast of a man beside him. "We'll be in the corridor and not one step farther."

Nim was grateful because she'd no idea how many of Warrick's men were aware of his situation. Even fewer, she suspected, were aware of hers. All she could think of was how many times she'd exposed Warrick to their scrutiny since she'd met him, how many times he'd had to save her from the Trust. It was just what the Trust wanted, a threat to Warrick, something they could use against him. Nim kept playing into their hands.

When Maris rushed into the room and the guards had moved outside, Nim explained to Margery how Warrick had made a sacrifice to protect Wesley from magic.

"No one can use magic on him?"

"No," Wes told her. "None but Warrick himself."

Margery's gaze was calculating, but there was no time for lengthy debate.

"Someone in that hall has magic," Nim said. *Rhen*, her mind supplied. *It was Rhen. It was Rhen. It was Rhen.* And he was coming back for her. She shook herself. "If Warrick's powers are revealed..."

"Well, you can't go back," Margery snapped. "That was a warning for you, and we all know it. Lora isn't a threat to anyone, let alone the higher-ups at the Trust."

A sickness swam in Nim's gut at the remembered sight of the woman's bloody wound. "So what, then? We do nothing? Let them play their games?"

"After the king's announcement, I presume their game is about to get a fair deal more dangerous." Margery's mouth was turned down, and her eyes pinched. She was working very hard on some problem, if Nim knew that look at all.

"They aren't allowed in the castle," Wes said. "If someone got in—"

"Rhen has proven that he doesn't care about rules," Nim reminded him.

At the mention of his name, Maris, previously watching the exchange with unease, flinched.

Nim narrowed a look at her. "What do you know?"

She shook her head, but Nim wasn't certain whether she knew nothing or did not want to speak of it. Many in Inara refused even to utter the name of the Trust, should the calling of it bring dark fates upon them.

Nim thought it was a little too late for that from one of her personal guards, but she didn't say so. She crossed her arms. "I thought we were done with lying."

The maid stared back for a long moment then said, "Only talk among the guard that the younger heir has a bit of a penchant for"—her mouth shifted as if tasting the word—"as you say, my lady, for games."

Her tone made clear that the sort of games he enjoyed made Calum's look like child's play.

"So our choice is... what? Stay here and hope whatever maneuvering the Trust is about does not reach us or go out in search of trouble that we are certain is there?"

They were trapped in the sitting room with no escape aside from a secret passageway Nim should certainly not share with Margery and possibly not Maris or the corridor full of guards outside.

"You should not leave, my lady." Maris's words dragged Nim's attention back to the woman. It was not as if she'd read her thoughts but that Nim had escaped the last time Warrick had attempted to keep her in his rooms, and Maris well knew it. But then Nim felt the sudden, inescapable pull of magic, too powerful, calling her to it.

"They're together." Nim's words slipped free, and all eyes shot to hers. Fingers fumbling in her pocket, she drew out one of the vials Allister had given her and downed the tonic. It hurt. She winced, shook her head, and pointedly did not explain that she could feel that Warrick and his brother had come so close, together in a way that made it impossible to resist their draw.

"Who?" Margery demanded, but Nim could not bring herself to say it aloud.

Two sons of the powerful queen. Together. She knew it was Rhen with Warrick, even though she'd still not managed to discern between the sense of Rhen and of Calum. Fates save her, she didn't want to think about what should happen if all three were ever to gather at once. She shook off a chill at the thought and realized Wes's hand was on her, scarred beneath a pair of fine gloves and protecting her from any harm the magic might have done to her. Wesley might keep it from touching her, but she didn't think he could fathom how the magic could harm her in other, less tangible ways.

Nim's heart raced with the need to act. She should have run, hidden, taken the others somewhere safer, far away from the warning pull of the magic. But every part of her shoved in a foolish direction—toward the draw where the brothers faced off. Because they had to have been facing off. Neither Rhen nor Calum were welcome inside the castle outside of the king's dungeons, and the last time Rhen had seen Warrick, he'd called him "brother" in front of the king's men.

Her knees went weak, and her stomach swam. If Warrick's connection to the Trust was revealed in a room filled with courtiers, with officers of the court, he would be hanged—worse than hanged, surely, though she could not think of precisely what that fate might entail.

"Nim." Wes's words were close, a bit unsteady and terror-stricken, like she was. Only the others did not know what was happening, the truth of how horrible it was. She pressed her hand tightly to her stomach and forced herself to focus on her surroundings. Somehow, she'd moved to the door and pressed one hand hard against it. She had to go to Warrick and to the source of the draw.

"It has to be done," Margery said a second before a cold basinful of water was tossed at Nim's face.

She gasped, eyes wide.

Margery set the basin down and gave her a measuring stare. Maris stood beside her, hand on the hilt of a sword in a sheath strapped around her waist. Nim was not alone. She had people willing to fight for her and with her to stand against the Trust. They would keep her from doing the bidding of the magic's call.

Nim straightened her shoulders then gave a sharp nod to the lot of them. And then a concussion from a blast of power exploded through the room—or through Nim, because apparently no one else seemed to notice. She was knocked into Wesley, who caught and steadied her before she shoved off him and wrenched open the door.

She had to find Warrick.

She rushed into the corridor, only to meet a wall of the king's men standing guard. But Maris was at her back, and with a quick gesture, the petite lady's maid who was no simple maid at all ordered the guards aside. Nim's slippered feet moved swiftly over the stone floor. Maris and Wesley were on either side of her as the others followed. When they turned the last corner to the gathering hall, the corridor was filled with men, king's guard, courtiers, and officers of the court.

All turned to stare at her. Nim fell to a stop just as Maris slipped an arm through hers to conceal her longsword between their skirts. Suddenly and painfully aware there was no commotion among the lot of them, that no one had felt the concussion but her and that she'd just run into the corridor after being well and truly doused with a basinful of water, Nim drew a sharp breath and ran a hand over her bodice. Fates save her, but she could not comport herself even when her life actually relied on it.

The crowd shifted, half the group turning from their gawking of her as they made way for a small group exiting the gathering hall. *Warrick*. He was safe. Shoulders square and coronet in place, he strode through the crowd and into her view as if nothing were amiss. Then he seemed to notice that those around him had been ruffled, and his gaze rose to find the source.

An intimation of his surprise shot through her, followed by mingled relief and concern. All of this happened as Nim stood damp and panting, bookended by a sword-wielding lady's maid, the seneschal's messenger, and a pack of guards at their back—a tableau of peculiarity if not impropriety.

Warrick seemed to take in the potential for it to become a predicament just as Margery joined the group—she'd always been oddly poor at running—and he approached with a louder than strictly necessary "Ah, Wesley, thank you for fetching our new constable with such haste." His eyes flicked to Nim's. "Lady Weston, if you please."

Warrick gestured toward the corridor in the opposite direction from which he'd come and gave a clipped order to Wesley to fetch the summons from the table in his study. As Warrick strode past, Nim managed to incline her head gently then turn to follow without glancing back at the watching crowd. They made their way to an empty sitting room, where he finally faced what was left of the group. "Maris, please see that Lady Margery is returned to the safety of her manor." When she gave a quick nod, his attention shifted to Margery. "Lady Margery, your assistance is greatly appreciated, as always. You have my thanks as well as Inara's, regardless of whether they realize how you've been of aid."

Margery curtsied deeply. "Your lordship, it's been my pleasure." The tilt to her mouth said she only ever did what gave her pleasure, regardless of whether the court cared. Her dark eyes came to Nim's, sparking with a secret smile. "Nimona. Until next time."

Once they were gone and Nim and Warrick were finally alone, he turned to her with a solemn expression.

"What happened?" she asked.

He shook his head. "Nothing of consequence. It's sorted now, and that's what matters. We can discuss the rest later." What he didn't say was that there was something far more pressing he needed to do, which could not wait a moment longer. She narrowed her gaze at him, and the line of his mouth tightened. "Come along," he told her. He snatched a small towel from a side table and passed it to her, nothing coming from him but lingering warmth from the magic and a too-vague intimation.

They exited the sitting room through an opposite door, and Warrick walked beside her at an entirely respectable distance as she dabbed water from her neck and jaw. It had been mere moments since the gathering had been released, but the corridors were lined only with guards, quiet of the earlier commotion and traffic. They passed through several doorways, another long corridor, and into a section of the castle Nim did not recall.

Warrick paused before the entrance to what appeared to be the central tower then gestured for her to go before him. She stared into the narrow passage as he took a torch from the wall and lit a flame with his magic. The light was strong and steady as they moved upward to an unknown destination that she only knew for certain Warrick was eager to reach. Something had happened with Rhen, unquestionably, and it made whatever they were about to do more pressing. It felt like a thousand steps through the winding stairwell, the air still and close with early summer heat, but his urgency was seeping into her emotions and driving her faster toward their destination.

The stairs ended at a small landing with a few crates stacked near a barred door and little else. Warrick's mouth twitched at the look Nim gave him, but he walked past her to unbar the door. It opened to a shock of fresh air and a dark sky. He took her hand, tossed the towel aside, and led her to stand before a crenellated wall with him. She drew in a sharp breath.

They stood atop the tower, staring out over all of Inara. Warrick's hand slipped from hers, and a familiar warmth swelled through her as the clouds parted and moonlight painted the stone of the castle and a sea of rooftops with its silvery glow. Beyond the walls, she could make out forests, and farther still, the shape of the mountains that bordered distant kingdoms. All around her were streets she'd known since she was a girl, familiar landmarks filled with memories both painful and sweet. It was Inara, her home. Silence wreathed her for a long moment, only the feel of the air on her skin and the view before her.

When Warrick finally spoke from beside her, his voice was soft. "No more waiting," he said. "The magistrate will meet us before the hour is gone."

His gaze roamed over her, his hand sliding across her waist as he shifted behind her. Nim finally understood why Maris had gone along with Margery's idea for a gown that was less appropriate for royal gatherings than a formal event. Maris had known —Warrick must have told her to prepare. And whatever had passed between he and the king made their union more urgent.

"I'm certain I look like a drowned rat," she said.

He leaned in to whisper against her ear. "Love"—his nose grazed her flesh and trailed lower. He paused to press a kiss to the delicate skin at the base of her neck—"you are ravishing."

She had the feeling he was not speaking of her dress. As Warrick stood behind her, his breath teasing her flesh in a way that sent pleasant shivers over her, Nim was reminded of the first night he'd touched her there, the night she'd received her scars, and the way his lips had pressed so gently to her skin. It was when she'd decided that she would stay, right before he'd knocked her out and hauled her to the bed of a wagon.

What are you thinking? he seemed to wonder.

Nim smiled. "Would that I could send you my very thoughts and emotions."

A chuckle rumbled through his chest where it pressed against her. "I'm not certain that would go well at all." She turned to face him, the smile still tilting her lips. She felt small in his arms, safe. Nim knew that Warrick had only meant to protect her when he'd forced her to leave, to do whatever he could to keep her and Wesley from harm. It wasn't his fault that she had fallen prey to his brother's games.

"I'm afraid you'll have to tell me," he said of her hidden thoughts.

She rose to her toes, brushing a light kiss over his lips. "I trust you," she promised. "And I swear my honor to you, before crown and kingdom, between earth and sky, from this breath to my last."

Warrick's own breath stilled at the familiar words, a section of the marriage vows spoken by all in Inara. He stared down at her and let the breath go, opening to her in a way he never had before. A wave of sensation flowed over her, so intense she could barely process it. He let her experience his need for her, his adoration, the way he'd felt the first time he'd seen her and the first time they'd touched.

Her heart squeezed, and something unfurled within her. The constant yearning she felt to brush against magic reached out to wrap about the power that swelled freely around her, the energy that was Warrick's. He was giving her access to all of him, leaving himself bare to her. It was a promise of what their bond would be and that the moment he was able, he would keep nothing from her at all.

If only they could complete the ceremony.

A sound echoed from behind the tower door, cutting through the intimations from Warrick with a sudden spike of alarm. Nim's mouth opened to ask what was wrong, but she knew. She could feel it from him.

No one should have known where they were.

CHAPTER 15

Wesley burst through the door, panting from what Nim could only assume was a frantic sprint up the ridiculously long stairwell. He fell to a stop at the sight of Warrick. "My lord," he managed before wheezing, "fate's sake."

"What is it?" Warrick snapped, impatient but not unkind.

Wes pressed a hand to his chest as he drew a deeper, gasping breath. "King's men intercepted the summons."

Heat seared through Warrick, but he only nodded. "Thank you for alerting me. You are not to blame for giving it up."

"I didn't." He drew the crumpled missive from his boot, finally settling into less ragged breaths. "Heard them coming from a corridor away." However proud he might have been by the action, Wes's expression remained disconsolate. "Magistrate is gone, though, called away on king's business."

Warrick's jaw went rigid, his hand tightening into a fist. "Where?"

Wes shook his head. "Don't know yet. I've set the guards on it, but no one expects her back soon. Word is her carriage was loaded with a trunk."

Resignation swam through Warrick as he pressed his fingers

to the bridge of his nose. After a moment, he sighed. "Thank you, Wes. Your attention to this matter is greatly appreciated." He placed a hand on the boy's shoulder. "Please escort the lady Nimona to my suite until I've had time to sort this out."

Wes gave a hesitant glance at the door to the stairwell. Nim bit her lip. Warrick gave him a pat. "Rest as long as you need. I'll return her on my way down." He held a hand out for Nim, and when she took it, she could only feel his regret and weariness.

"I'm sorry," she whispered when they were alone on the landing behind the closed door.

He brushed a thumb over her cheek, his intimation answering that it was only this *one* thing. If he could just have it done and keep her safe... They wouldn't have had to hide.

She stepped closer. "You've had to hide all along. I can endure this." She thought she could, in any case. She'd been hiding so much about herself since she was a girl, though, that truth be told, she wasn't certain how long she might manage endurance with the Trust and a king hunting her down.

He didn't want to make her. And he didn't want to for himself.

"Warrick," she said, "how did you come to be seneschal?" Right beneath everyone's nose, she meant. If he was truly to be hidden, far from Inara might have been the safest place. But she supposed the king might have wanted him near in his game with the head of the Trust. The king might have made a bargain.

Warrick's hand found hers, his thumb sliding over the delicate skin inside her wrist. "Stewart is cleverer than many give him credit for. He's not merely king in title. He has much experience in court maneuvering, relations between kingdoms, all that is required of a station so high." And in his dealings with the Trust.

"So by putting you at his hand..."

"Under his hand," he corrected.

Nim frowned. Warrick was not only bound by the laws of the kingdom but by whatever deal he'd made with Calum, a contract that apparently surpassed the wishes of his mother, if not the bonds of secrecy placed on him by the Trust. It begged the question of why he was so desperate to complete their ceremony—because if he and Nim were married, Warrick would be bound again, to her.

Her eyes met his. "That's it," she whispered. "The only way to put us before your other vows is to bind us legally." They needed to be bound by the laws of Inara and the laws of the Trust, besides that two agents of the king could not be seen lingering in stairwells like lovestruck fools.

"I tried to keep you safe," he reminded her. He stepped closer, his face lowering to keep his gaze on hers. "Neither of us are able to heed the good sense of holding our distance, it seems." It was barely a whisper that traced over her skin with a flutter of magic.

"Indeed." Her voice wasn't much more than a breath as Warrick drew closer to her, and any sense she might have possessed—good or otherwise—was well and truly lost to her.

Then the door rattled, and his eyes fell closed with tangible vexation.

"Oh," was all Wes said when he appeared on the landing. After a moment of silence, wherein his gaze traveled repeatedly between Warrick and Nim, who were blocking his way toward the stairwell, he said, "All rested up. I can take her now."

Warrick seemed to resist the urge to run a hand over his face. He let his gaze land on each of them. "Do stay out of trouble this time, the both of you."

Nim gave a sheepish shrug as Wes nodded at the request. And then Warrick was gone, turned to descend the darkened stairs at an improbable pace. Behind them, the torch flared to life again, the pulse of the magic beating with Nim's own heart. Wesley took the torch in hand before sidling up to her. "Ready?"

They'd managed to escape for a moment. At her nod, they began their descent into a reality Nim was not quite ready to face.

Nim paced Warrick's suite, plucking the lids off various containers and decorative boxes to peer inside and running her fingers over the edges of trim. She arranged the fruit on his table then straightened his writing supplies on his desk. She drew the poker from its place by the hearth, raising it to eye level before testing the thing's balance. It wasn't half bad.

"You're restless," Wes said.

She put the poker back in its spot.

"Why don't we go out to the gardens?" he offered.

She blinked at him then gestured to the tall rows of windows outside, where it was fully dark.

"Cards?"

Flopping into the chair with a sigh, she asked, "How am I to relax when there is so much to be done? We are meant to lounge around a set of locked rooms and do nothing to prevent what might come, and I loathe it, Wes. I truly do."

Wes blew out a breath. "Would you rather work, then?"

She sat up. "Can we?"

"We can't go to your study, but a few reports did come in. I was to deliver them in the morning."

"Yes," she said. "That. Please let us do *anything* other than wait idly to be attacked."

He gave her a look but stood to retrieve the documents.

Nim wasted no time lighting a few tapers from the sitting room and spreading them over Warrick's fine desk. She gestured to Wes to draw up a chair, and they began to scan through the information she'd requested of Lord Preston and his associates. Half at least were connected with the city watch. Another few held posts outside the wall, and least connected but most worrisome was a king's messenger who had carried missives as far as other kingdoms.

Lord Preston's involvements appeared to be in a rather unseemly set, at best, should he have had any ties to the Trust.

At worst, he could be the very person Calum had put in position to take Warrick's place as heir. She needed to verify exactly how the succession would go. Surely, the rules were not secreted, even if the man's lineage was. *I'll see you again*, Rhen had said, *soon*.

Wesley glanced up at Nim's murmured curse.

"We need to send a message to Margery," she said.

"Right now?"

"You do it for seneschal business."

"Yes, but Warrick doesn't give a whit whether his recipients are awake and receiving guests."

Nim grinned. "Margery keeps late hours. And early ones. Honestly, I'm not certain when she even sleeps." She patted Wes's hand. "Besides, she'll strangle us if we don't let her know right away."

Wes didn't ask what it was precisely that they were informing Margery of, but Nim assumed that was a habit he'd gained from being Warrick's messenger. The boy probably knew as much about Lord Preston as anyone, and she would do well to remember his time in the castle and among the court—he was one of her most advantageous resources.

But Maris knocked at the door to the sitting room, bearing a tray with a very late dinner. "The seneschal asked that I ensure you both were fed."

"Right." Nim scratched a hasty note to Margery as Wesley joined Maris in the sitting room, snatching two rolls and a hunk of meat from the tray on his way past. When Nim finally finished the missive, two pages long, she made her way to the sitting room to deliver it to him.

He took it and gave the lady's maid a look. "She's not to leave this room."

Maris inclined her head slightly but instead of the expected "as you say," she replied, "I wouldn't dream of letting her."

Wes's answering grin seemed to imply it was a mite trickier than all that, but he let it go, giving them both a small wave before heading out the door.

"Maris," Nim said as she stood in the center of the sitting room, "if whatever threat there was earlier is resolved, why is it, I wonder, that I am not allowed to leave without Wesley?"

"Is there somewhere else you wish to be, my lady?"

Nim pursed her lips. She supposed not. If anything, she should return to her work at Warrick's desk. But when she gave a nod of acquiescence, Maris did not follow into Warrick's study, and it was only a reminder that Nim was in the seneschal's private rooms, as if nothing was untoward, as if it was not an act that could deem them both unfit to conduct themselves as agents of the king.

It did nothing to stop her from completing her work, and in the small hours before dawn, Nim was awakened by the gentle touch of that very seneschal's hand as he brushed a thumb across her cheek.

She shot up, parchment plastered to her face and ink across her fingertips. Warrick's brow rose, but all she felt from him was warmth. She ran a hand over her face and pointedly did not look at the mess she'd made of his desk. "Did you fix it?"

His intimations drew back as he shook his head. "Come to bed, love. You can worry about the rest in the morning."

"But—"

He reached a hand down to hers. "Maris has returned to your rooms. When dawn comes, you can take the hidden corridor to rejoin her." He stared down at her. "I only want to hold you for a while and rest with you safe at my side."

Nim stood to follow, but she did not like what it meant that he had no simple answer. Warrick was losing his battle over her with the king.

CHAPTER 16

Rhen's threats did not seem as if they might let up. The next day, Nim strolled a courtyard garden with Maris, taking in the sun between her hours in the dim study of her new post. When she was drawn to a particularly stunning rose bush, she leaned forward, unaware in the moment precisely what the draw meant. She only moved toward it, unable to stop herself from touching the soft petals, heedless of all else around her.

Then Maris's blade cut the air before her, hard and fast like a serpent's strike.

Nim drew in a sharp breath and glanced down as horror rose in her like a tide. The body of a long black snake spilled blood onto the paving stones inches from her feet, split into two separate pieces by the blade of a queen's protector.

It had been bad, absolutely, but late that night, when Nim went to the passageway to seek out Warrick in his rooms, she paused in the darkness, more than a little aware of the slithering, unpleasant sort of magic with her in the corridor. Another serpent had found her—another warning from Rhen. Nim's hand flew to her dagger, but she did not strike. She took the coward's way and slunk back into her room, where she proceeded to lock herself away until morning.

She did so with a commitment that had Maris on notice. Nothing could be done for it. Rhen's warnings had been clear and did not bode well for what was to come at the public ball, yet the king was out for Nim's blood. There would be precious few chances to search out Lord Preston and answers to what the Trust had planned.

"My lady," Maris finally said. When Nim's head snapped up, Maris explained, "The lady Margery has arrived."

Margery bustled into the room with an armful of documents and garments. "Alice?"

The girl beamed at Nim. "Your ladyship," she started, but she was so laden with garment bags that she was unable to perform a proper curtsy.

"What are you doing?" Nim hissed at her friend.

Margery only shrugged. "Well, I can't very well bring in someone who doesn't know your precious secrets, now can I?" She dropped her burden onto a table. "And we need help."

"We?"

She gave Nim a look. "We. And when you explained how things worked with Wesley, well, honestly, what harm could come from having double that sort of protection? Besides, it's not as if I can trust my own help with it. That lot has no skill at holding their tongues, and you know it."

Nim gaped at her. She wasn't wrong about what Alice could do, precisely, but using her to shield themselves from magic was not the same as using Wes. The seneschal's messenger was already involved. "She's just a girl."

Alice's posture went rigid. "My lady. I am an agent of the king. This is king's business, is it not?"

"No!" Nim shouted. Fate's sake, the king wanted her dead. "And I'm not about to involve you in it." She turned to glare at Margery, so when a low voice sounded at her ear, she nearly jumped from her skin.

"To be fair, while she does believe she's about important business for the constable, mostly, she's just loyal to you, my lady. To a fault, possibly, but it remains unchangeable."

"Allister." Nim gasped and turned, finding her erstwhile valet dressed in a suit fit for royalty.

"We're to assist you to the ball, my lady, if you'll have us."

"Whether you'll have them or not," Margery snapped. "Don't pretend they're in less danger alone at Hearst Manor than here, under the protection of the castle guard. Now come. We've not much time."

THE NIGHT'S ball was an annual celebration, a nod to the tradition of chasing birds from early summer crops. While the children who performed the seasonal work were likely at home in their beds, society had bedecked themselves in lavish gowns and feathered masks, bells and strings of noisemakers in delicate glass and metal chiming at every arch and doorway. Music swelled through the space with the muffled swish of fabric, the scents of sweet foods overwhelmed by heady incense, its smoke coiling through the air like so many snakes.

Nim's heart was in her throat. "This was a horrible idea."

Margery patted a hand on Nim's arm where it laced through hers. "Pshaw. Masques are never a horrible idea."

Nim turned to glare, but the feathers jutting from her mask stole any gravity from the threat. Margery's mask was a sleek, catlike thing, formed to her face in a way that made her somehow more menacing and captivating at once. "How are we to find anyone when we can't see who they are?"

"My friend, some days, you lack imagination entirely." Margery's lip curled into a smile as she released Nim's arm to take Alice's. "Now, dance with Allister and see how long that dress of yours takes to snare some prey."

Nim let her breath go then wiped a palm over the material of her skirt and took Allister's proffered hand.

"My lady," he said. "Exceptionally hideous scheme, as one might come to expect."

A helpless laugh escaped her, but she inclined her head in agreement and walked with him onto the dance floor, in the posture of a proper lady. Allister's practiced ease at such things allayed much of her distress, but the ballroom was crowded with high society and all that it entailed. Nim did not like being unable to see what was coming for her, who was swirling by in layers of silk and jewels, or what slithering, shadowed things might be waiting beneath her feet. But she felt none of the warnings she'd tried so hard to stay alert to, no draw in any particular direction, no chill that urged her to run.

She only felt the unpleasantness of being surrounded by a society that had ousted her as a girl.

She stumbled, missing a step, and Allister steadied her to deftly recapture their rhythm. Nim did not excel at dancing. She'd had lessons as a girl but hadn't much occasion to use them since. Allister led her skillfully, his expression entirely solemn beneath a slender fox mask and short, dark hair.

"Look at us," she murmured, "the fox and the hen."

His lip twitched, but his expression did not falter. "A grand pair."

"I've missed you," she said.

His chin dipped just a fraction. "The manor has not been the same without your presence, my lady."

She drew a steadying breath, letting it out at an angle to blow a feather away from her face and survey the crowd past Allister's shoulder. Curses, but he was tall.

He spun them, as if reading her thoughts, and the crowd seemed to part against the far wall, where, away from the king's table and all his royal guests, a graceful man stood in black robes, an unadorned mask covering him from brow to nose.

Warrick. She could feel it. His eyes were on her as they spun again, and Allister's steady steps led her, though her gaze continued to seek out the seneschal. The music changed then rose again, and they danced into the crowd, his maneuvering of her keeping them distant enough not to brush other couples but near, should she decide to actually focus on her task and seek out Lord Preston and his associates. She let her attention swim past the faces, painted and masked as they were. She knew something of the man's build, thanks to Margery's reconnaissance, but she wondered if he would so openly risk mingling with suspicious characters at a king's ball. She wondered if she would be able to sense magic near him or how close she might have to get. He would need to hide it, surely, even if the king could not sense it himself. He would have been a fool to be so brazen.

Someone *had* attacked during a gathering, it was true, but that had been intentional, a warning. If the man hadn't been caught after years beneath the king's watch, then Nim and her friends had little chance of rooting him out quickly. And Nim didn't know whether the king was aware who was in place, only that he would not suffer anyone with ties to the Trust to remain. There was no telling whether he had been keeping the man near, just as he'd tried to outwit the head of the Trust when it came to heirs.

Allister leaned closer. "Your frown wounds a man's pride, my lady."

She let out a huff of laughter and glanced back at him. He was entirely stately, even in costume dress. "What are we all playing at, Allister? This will never work."

He drew her in a sidestep to bring them closer to a wall lined with tables. "Perhaps the lady Margery merely fancied a ball."

Doubtful. Margery hated the frippery of court gatherings. "It was nice of her to at least let Alice participate in the festivities, now that we've endangered her with the rest. Do you think she's enjoying herself?"

Allister spun, facing Nim at a slight and wide-eyed figure with light-auburn braids coiled at the base of her neck, dancing with a man wearing a crow headpiece who absolutely towered over her. Nim grinned, and Allister brought them finally to the edge of the ballroom, giving her a bow worthy of the most proper gentlemen. "And what have we learned?" he asked her.

She shrugged. "That masked balls are meant for dancing, not for scouting marks."

"As you say—" he started but was cut off by Margery tugging his tailcoat.

"Come," she ordered. "I've changed my mind. She'll not snare a lord of any kind with you milling about, handsome as you are. Dance with me instead."

Allister gave Nim a look that barely skirted formality before nodding his farewell as Margery dragged him back onto the floor. Nim found Alice again, dancing with a new partner, and Lady Constance, who wore a jeweled headpiece that might barely have been considered a mask, as it covered only part of a single brow. Nim took a glass from the table, emptied it, and let her gaze search out Warrick again.

He had moved closer and stood among a group of courtiers but kept his eyes on her. He had no intention of letting her out of his sight, apparently, after what had happened at the gathering. Nim bit her lip. It seemed unlikely that a seneschal could truly be disguised by only a half mask. Surely, if she knew who he was, then the rest of the courtiers did as well. Margery twirled into Nim's line of sight with Allister, blocking view of Warrick with a gesture that said it was time to do her job. She was to find Lord Preston and track who he made time with. Aside from Warrick watching her every move, Nim's heart wasn't in it. The problem of the Trust felt so big, so impossible to overcome.

Since she was a girl, she had wanted her freedom. But when Warrick had broken her contract and given her the thing she'd been so determined to fight for, Nim had realized she could never leave Inara and abandon those she loved to the Trust and their tortures. So she was stuck, not entirely returned to good society but in its very midst, pinned between a king who wanted her hanged and the head of the Trust, who wanted her for something worse.

Her choices warred with each other. The Trust's secrets kept them protected, and until she found a way to distance herself from them, she would never be safe from the king. She could not beat the Trust on her own, not when the undercity was filled with those who held magic, untold numbers against one reckless woman.

But she wasn't alone any longer. Margery's father had been taken by the Trust. Allister's charge, the gentleman Hearst, was gone. How many others, she couldn't guess, but Nim had friends. She had Warrick. She just needed to figure out how to use the help to gain security against something that felt insurmountable.

"My lady," a man beside her in a raven mask said. He held his hand toward her, and despite the urge to draw away, Nim forced herself to take it. She owed at least that much to Margery, no matter how wrong it felt to play along with the courtiers who had disowned her.

As the man led her to the dance floor, Nim caught sight of Wesley, unmasked and in his capacity as official messenger. He darted between the couples at the edge of the room, finding Warrick with surprising skill. She supposed he'd had some experience seeking him out in crowds, and besides, it hadn't taken Nim long, either. Her partner spun her in the opposite direction, and though he was a perfectly adequate dancer, he was not Allister, so her misstep tripped them both.

He gave her a bit of space and waited two beats before picking up the steps again. Nim's gaze went back to Warrick. Wesley gestured, leaned in to speak privately, then led Warrick across the ballroom. She searched for Margery and Allister, finding them with Alice near a group of courtiers and a table of wine. When she looked back, Warrick was leaving the ballroom with more haste than she liked. Nothing felt off—nothing felt magical or wrong. It was likely king's business and nothing else. Surely.

Nim tried to see past her dance partner to the king's table. Stewart was sitting with a half dozen advisers, listening stone-faced as they appeared to jest and tell stories. At least his eyes were not on her. She sighed then returned her attention to her dance partner, who seemed not to have noticed it had ever been elsewhere.

They glided farther into the crowd, and as the music changed, Nim was handed off to a man wearing a dark wolf mask. She'd worn gloves for the evening, as was commonly done at balls, but the hand that slipped into hers was bare. Unease skittered over her flesh, and Nim let her gaze trail from the long fingers wrapping about her gloves to the dark eyes set deep inside the mask. They crinkled up at the edges as if in a smile, and it felt as if the floor had dropped from beneath her feet.

The wolf was Rhen.

CHAPTER 17

"Draw notice, and it will cost you that lovely neck." He leaned in to whisper, "And not just yours, I'll wager. Imagine the response to the high seneschal being revealed as one of us—Inara's most reviled of enemies." *A magic user*, he thought at her with a shiver of mock revulsion.

Frozen in his grip, she felt the shiver tremble over her own skin. His thoughts were too close, coming too rapidly and seeming so real that they felt nearly like hers, tangling in her emotions and sparking a desire to act. She needed space from him. She needed *away*.

She couldn't move.

Behind the mask, Rhen smiled. She felt that too. He knew he had her. *Snared*, one of them thought. She wasn't sure who.

Her chest rose and fell beneath a bodice that suddenly felt painfully tight, but the rest of her was at his mercy. The magic she'd not sensed before swam suddenly around her, as if he'd somehow hidden it until he desired her to know he was there. Her eyes wanted to dart around the room, to search for the help she'd been so sure of, but Nim was the only one who could sense the magic. And Warrick... fates, Warrick had been called from the ballroom.

Rhen chuckled at the nasty curse that slipped from her lips. "My lady, I *am* impressed."

"What are you doing here?" she hissed. She wasn't certain why she asked it, because if his plan was to hurt her, the last thing she should do was rush it along. But she hated being trapped and hated the feeling of his magic wrapped around her, binding her too tightly and holding her in place.

He sighed dramatically. "I do love a good ball." As the music rose, his hold on her eased, but only so that he might drag her with him in a mockery of dance. "And you, Lady Weston... what are *you* doing here?"

Nim stiffened at his intimation. Rhen knew the king wanted her gone, that she'd been threatened. He liked that she chose to come anyway, dancing before the king with only a feathered mask for protection and with an enemy of the kingdom, no less.

"I do see why my brothers are so enraptured by you. It's intoxicating, isn't it, the little amusements to be made with your position?" And her talent to let them inside her head and to sense when magic was being used against her.

He gave a satisfied little hum, as if thinking, but Nim could only shake her head violently. She couldn't stand it, couldn't seem to keep him out. The dagger was at her thigh, but there was little hope she could stab him in the center of the ballroom and not find herself and Warrick hanged by dawn. *Calum*, she realized. He was why Rhen was there. "We won't let him go." She sensed Rhen smiling at her again beneath his mask, but it was no longer pleasant. "He got what he deserved. Better than he deserved," she said. "And I won that contract as fairly as he won mine." Which was to say, not fairly at all.

"You think I desire the return of my eldest brother? That I would await his homecoming only to watch him take his place before me as heir?" Rhen laughed. "My dear, I am too clever for that by half."

She tried to jerk away from him but only managed to get herself bound tighter with magic. "Then why?" she snapped.

"What fool reason do you have to walk into the king's castle and parade about like you'll not be hanged just for being here?"

Will I? he seemed to think. *My brother has not been hanged.*

It was true. But Calum had been spared because he was bound under contract. The king had been able to lock him in a cell. He probably meant to use him in his battle against the Trust. And Warrick was the king's son.

Humor bubbled up from Rhen at the expressions crossing Nim's face. "Lady Weston, I do enjoy your company. But alas, you are correct. Our time is limited, and I should tell you why I've come."

Ice streaked up her spine. Rhen had been in her rooms, in the corridors, in the castle gardens. None of what he said could be trusted. He did not play by the rules, and she could not allow herself to forget it.

He leaned closer, his mask seeming to writhe until she blinked and shook his thoughts away. His voice was low and careful, not the playful tone he'd used before. "I am here to make an offer for you, my lady." She stared back at him, vaguely aware they'd stopped moving, that the press of the crowd around them seemed to ebb, and no one else in the room had noticed their presence. All she felt was Rhen's magic and the thin silver band on her finger.

A chuckle rumbled from him at her reaction. "Oh, my lady. But wouldn't that be delightful? I see my mistake." He shifted straighter, still holding her, the two of them standing as if frozen mid-dance. "Just a bargain, you see? Far less dreadful than a proposition, in my opinion."

"I don't make bargains." The response came as a reflex, too loud despite that the dancers surrounding them gave no sign of notice.

Rhen's eyes narrowed behind the mask. "But you do, when it is to save someone you love."

Nim felt the words like a slap, still unable to tear from his grip. She opened her mouth to reply, but she'd no interest in reminding him that he did not have to make her agree, that Calum had only tricked her, stolen her blood, and bound her against her will. Her voice went cold. "My father is dead. That bargain did not save him at all."

With a sound of assent, he spun them a half turn and said, "Regardless, I think you will want to hear this one out."

The fear in her had only grown as her shock subsided, and Nim had a very bad feeling about his offer even before he laid it out. Her gaze searched the crowd, but she could see none of her friends, only a wall of dancing courtiers, masked and oblivious to the danger right beside them.

"You know we will win," Rhen said. "The game is only sport." He waited until her eyes returned to his. "You know we are patient, that we have time to let our stratagem play out. I will not even ask much of you."

She glared.

He grinned. "Let me keep you," he said. "A trophy to hold over both my brothers." As she tried to jerk away, he added, "And in return, you will be left alive."

Nim stilled. If she didn't do what he wanted, he meant to kill her, right there on the ballroom floor.

The dagger was warm against her leg. She pressed a hand to her stomach, feeling honestly as if she might retch, but Rhen moved closer before she could make a move for her weapon. "Ah-ah," he murmured. "You've stabbed me once, Miss Weston. Best not to add to your debt."

Her gaze shot to his.

"That's right," he told her. "Has my brother not explained the rules?" He *tsked* when she went pale. "So many bindings placed on my brothers. Rules upon rules." She could feel his words go slick with his smile. "Though I am not above making use of a few of them when it benefits me."

It seemed as if Rhen had held her captive for an age, but the song changed, and she knew it had only been tortuously long minutes. "My contract is broken. I am no longer beholden to your rules," she said.

He liked the way her voice quavered, and he let her feel him relish it. "It does not signify. You see, my lady, you drew the blood of an agent of the Trust, an heir no less, inside the under-city. I don't have to tell you that citizens of Inara are not under the kingdom's protection there, but still, I doubt this king is willing to risk war to save a woman with ties to the Trust. You shall pay for your crime." His grip on her tightened. "And if you do not, it is my right to claim recompense on the one whose magic was threaded through that dagger."

Nim's knees gave out, but Rhen held her firm. "So you see," he said. "That is the bargain I offer. It is you, or it is Warrick."

Nim did not miss the echo of Warrick's offer from the first night they'd met—a bargain he had never sealed with magic and that had tied her only by threat. But Rhen was not Warrick. He was not asking her to risk being hanged, he was forcing her to choose between her own life and Warrick's, between herself and the future of the kingdom. She could not.

Fates, but she couldn't even make herself consider the possibility that it might be the choice her father's bargain had led her to... a choice she would not make.

Her expression firmed in her resolution, but before she could spit back "never," Rhen tipped his mask up to reveal a calculating grin. Nim's heart skipped. He bared his face to the ballroom, to the king, as he danced with *her*.

Throat tight, as if the coming noose had already cinched her neck, she stared back at the man who had just seen her hanged.

He leaned close, holding her trapped by magic, his lips a blade's breadth from her ear. "Time's up."

Stones rumbled beneath Nim's feet as Rhen's pleasure swam through her, but it was not his magic she felt. It was a hot, roiling thing, staggering in its intensity. Warrick knew Rhen was there. Warrick had seen him, holding her, his jaw at her neck, his bare hands tight on her flesh.

Warrick was coming.

He knew what Rhen had done. Rhen gave Nim a parting smile, and the instant his grip let go, she hit the floor. Her limbs were useless, her body a river of sensations, none of them good. She was being dragged under by the magic, too much at once, too close, and yet, Rhen was gone. Above her, the crowd seemed to come to their senses. A hush fell around her, followed by the settling of fabric and the stuttering death of the orchestra music. The distant realization passed through her mind that maybe some of them had not noticed that she'd danced with an heir to the Trust in front of a king, but it was gone too quickly. Shoving past the stunned onlookers, Warrick broke into the small space where she lay. His fury was tangible, beneath it, fear and dread. Indecision. He needed to help her, to keep her from the king's hands. He could not do so without defying the laws of the kingdom. He had to pursue Rhen.

Worse, those around them were clearly beginning to suspect that something more had happened. Margery pushed past a short woman in a dove mask as Warrick knelt beside Nim. He had not seemed to decide whether he might carry her to safety or if he would seize her as if she'd performed a criminal act. He only needed her out of the ballroom. A look passed between Margery and Warrick, then he stood, his voice not quite steady as he commanded the festivities to resume. Just a swoon, someone in the crowd said, as if ladies did so all the time and as if they had not noticed the magic or the agent of the Trust. The onlookers shifted, some going back to their conversations, others watching in wait. Surely, no one had forgotten what had happened to Lady Lora only days before. Surely, they realized something was terribly wrong. Nim couldn't have been the only person who had felt the magic raging through the room.

She wasn't able to see the dais but could sense from Warrick that the king looked on, a cold promise in his gaze. Stewart flicked a gesture to the men beside him, and Warrick flinched. "Move," he told Margery.

He was breaking the rules, interfering with a king's command.

Margery gave a sharp nod, then she and Allister lifted Nim as Alice dug through a pocket on her costume gown and retrieved a vial.

Nim lost a moment to the effects of the magic, and then they were in the corridor, smelling salts beneath her nose. She choked, wheezed a curse, and closed her eyes for a long, horrible moment. When she opened them again, the lot of them were in Nim's room. Alice scurried about while Allister and Margery settled Nim onto her bed. They were fussing with her shoes, loosening her bodice. Her mask had been lost, and her fingers were cold. Maris waited at the foot of the bed, watching. A line of blood crossed the maid's knuckles.

Nim was not bleeding.

Her eyes met Maris's. Something had happened. Perhaps she'd fought to reach Nim beyond the crowd. Perhaps Rhen had distracted the lady's maid the way he had Warrick.

"Stop," Nim said to the others. "I'm not hurt. Please." She waved away their ministrations. "Just leave me be for a moment." Fates take it, she was done for. It might not happen in the next moment, but by dawn, when his guests had left, the king would summon her. Not for a visit. Not for a cell.

Alice settled a teacup and plate onto the bedside table.

Nim's throat felt tight. She had lost. She'd no idea how she'd ever thought she could win a game in which she was only a pawn. She was powerless. "Thank you," she told them, her voice breaking. "Thank you all, but please... I need to be alone."

Margery and Maris gave Nim a look, but Allister inclined his head, and when he turned to go, Alice followed. The other two eventually did the same, not bothering to conceal their dissent.

Nim stared at the canopy of her massive bed for what felt

like hours, but it was not hours. Time was crawling. Her scar throbbed, and her limbs felt weak. She needed rest, but there was no chance she would actually find sleep. If she could walk down to the dungeons and bloody Calum with her mace, it might help. Or if she could go back to when she'd stabbed Rhen and do a better job of it. Those were the things that would ease her. Those or the company of Warrick and knowing that he was safe.

His magic hit her, warm and strong but not near. She sat up, shaking off a sensation that the room spun, and tugged her bodice back into place. Hiking the skirt of her gown, Nim made quick work of removing the scabbard from her thigh to strap it instead at the ready on her waist. She wasn't certain what she was about—it was not as if she could take down the entire king's guard when they came for her—but she could not allow herself to feel any more helpless than she already did. The door to the sitting room was closed, her friends waiting beyond it. They were loyal and trustworthy and not at all equipped to help her evade a noose. She took a taper from the mantel and followed the feel of magic into the hidden passageway. It did not lead her to Warrick's rooms.

Instead, the maze of passages took her through the castle and out a slim panel into a room she'd never before visited. It was furnished in rich wood, dimly lit by the glow of a wall trench with not a single window to reveal the night sky. At its center stood Warrick, eyes downcast and hand on his sword. Nim crossed the space to him, seeing only a pair of chaises, a small table stacked with long-forgotten books, a desk, and a bed.

Expression dark, he did not turn to her as she stopped beside him but continued to stare toward the space that held the bed. It was there, at his side and the familiar vantage point, that Nim recognized the room. The bed was new, and she'd only seen the space in vague intimations, but the memory struck her hard because it meant something to Warrick.

He was standing where he had watched a woman burn. Nim pressed a hand to her mouth, but it didn't cover the sound that rose from her. Warrick drew a breath, his hold on the intimations cracking. He'd been so young, and Stewart so determined. It had felt as if there were no other way. The king had tried to hide the women from the head of the Trust, to steal them into the castle and keep them locked away so that they might marry the king and bring into the world a legitimate heir.

An heir who was not Warrick.

"This is what she does," the king had said. "Look at how she plagues us. You, me, the kingdom. Fates take her, but she plagues my very soul."

And they had watched as the body of another would-be queen turned to cinder by magic-bought flame, knowing full well that every mysterious illness and every accident was another move made by the head of the Trust in her game. Another way to keep a king's hands tied, to bring her children into power and crush the bargains they'd made to keep Inara safe.

Nim's hands were trembling, her knees unsteady. They all kept thinking of it as a game, but what the Trust was planning was far worse than anything of the sort. Warrick seemed to bring himself to awareness as he slid an arm around her. "I'm sorry," he said. "Sorry for the danger I've put you in, that I cannot seem to keep you safe." For what he would have to do before morning. They crumpled together onto a chaise a few steps away. Knowing what Warrick had been through as a child did not compare to feeling his memory of it, taking in the pain it still caused him. "To see his hands on you." Warrick's voice was rough, and he seemed unable to say Rhen's name. "How close he came to you, that he threatened you in your very home." His words fell away, but the intimation went on. Rhen had destroyed any chance Nim had of being returned to the king's service. He had called out Warrick in front of the guard, called him "brother."

She rested her hand on Warrick's chest and pressed her forehead to his. "How do you live with this?" The torment that seethed in him, she meant, the constant worry and the memories.

He kept it put away, locked in the depths of his heart with all the other things the head of the Trust could not be allowed to touch. Warrick's hand came to rest over hers, his intimations coming more freely, confessions in answer to her question. He had been so young then, just a child. He had not truly understood.

Stewart had asked Warrick to take sacrifices from him.

Nim went very still. There was no way to be certain what Warrick was allowed to reveal, as his secrets were bound by the Trust in ways beyond his vow of loyalty to the king. Still, such an admission, spoken aloud or not, felt dangerous.

"Sacrifices," she said.

His gaze met hers, their faces painfully close. "Not like yours."

A king would not be able to wear the scars that she and Warrick bore, markings that were recognizable to any who lived in Inara, lesions that told of magical encounters, something a king could never permit. He would have had to trade other things, things that mattered deeply, things that hurt to give.

"His hand. Fates, Warrick, he made you break his bones in sacrifice?"

Warrick did not answer but let go a shallow breath.

As a child, he'd had to torture his own father so that the man might keep Inara safe, a man who had done everything to find a way to bring another son—a true heir—into the world. For all that was sacred... Warrick's mother was a monster.

Nim's fingers wrapped tightly around his. Warrick bore scars far worse than those his brother had wrought on his flesh. She had known, but she had not understood the depths of it.

"I tell you this because I've no other choice," he admitted. "I can't stand by while they use you for their games. I won't—" His words cut off, but she felt the emotion in his silence. Fates, she did not know how he had withstood it. She only knew that it was worse because of her. Her safety was gone, their chance at a life ripped away.

Rhen had given her a choice: Warrick's freedom or hers.

To Nim, it was no choice at all.

CHAPTER 19

"They will come for you midday, when I am tied up by king's business. They plan to take you quietly." Warrick's words were calm and level, holding no hint of accusation that she'd kept Stewart's threat from him. He'd only returned her to her suite and stood before her, the report nothing as much as a vow. "We must wait until noontide, so they might believe we will not act against them, that we mean to hear the king's judgment." Warrick had no intention of doing so. He would have left with her right then if he thought he could get away with it. But the kingdom's eyes were upon him, and as seneschal, he had to secret her escape, to at least make an attempt at an alibi. For Inara. So that Stewart might keep his throne.

He stared at her for one long, heart-wrenching moment then pressed the softest kiss to her cheek, a promise that he would save her no matter the cost.

Nim stood, broken and spent, as he returned to the sitting room and her friends. Voices echoed through the doorway, turning her heart sick.

Allister's voice, too low and careful, as if he would not want her to hear, said, "...that I could offer a sacrifice... that she might become immune to the magic... in the way you have done for the others..." The others—Wesley and Alice.

Nim felt as if she was being crushed by the weight of all Inara.

Allister had offered to give a sacrifice so that Nim might be safe from magic. He had no idea how impossible it was.

The silence before Warrick's response was so long that Nim began to suspect he might not answer. When he did, it was with guarded words. Warrick could not reveal secrets that belonged to the Trust, no matter that they played a game with his life. "It cannot be done," he said. "Not by me. Not by anyone."

Because Nim was already bound. Until whatever bargain her father had made played out, Warrick could do nothing but try to keep her safe from the Trust and safe from the king.

Nim paced her room late into the night. Margery had returned to her manor, Alice and Allister to Hearst. She was alone with Maris outside in the sitting room and Warrick's personal guard at her door.

She had obsessed over every avenue, turned each possibility in her mind a thousand times. No matter how she examined the situation, Nim was left with one truth: the harder her opponents came after her, the more danger those she cared about would be in. Warrick, Wes, Allister. *Inara.* Everything because of her. Nim was the weakest point, the flaw in Warrick's armor. To the Trust, she was no more than a pawn. To the king, she was a danger to order and to his only son.

Stewart had lost his battles with the queen, no matter what he had tried. Warrick was the most important piece in the game, all that had and all that could keep Inara from Trust hands.

Rhen had given Nim an ultimatum. Unlike Calum, his motives had not been merely to tease and torment. Nim had found a slip of parchment in her pocket, so very like the ones she'd received with Calum's tasks. It had felt of Rhen, smelled of his person and his magic, and gave the sensation of fingers sliding over her skin. She had opened the folded parchment to reveal a message in what she could only assume was Rhen's hand: *Time's up.*

They were coming for Warrick before tomorrow's moon.

It was a warning that Rhen would not let her ignore his threat. Whatever Warrick had planned would not work. He might succeed in secreting her away or sneaking her out of Inara, but if Nim did not surrender herself to the Trust, they would come for Warrick to claim recompense for the magic Nim had used to wound Rhen and to destroy whatever chance he had of taking Stewart's place. Rhen would do it—she knew he would. He had already called Warrick "brother" in front of the king's guard, had walked into the ballroom and withdrawn his mask right under the king's nose.

He might have been enjoying it, but Rhen was not toying with any of them. He meant to tear Inara down.

❧

"My lady?" Wes's voice from the doorway was hesitant. It was barely past dawn, and he could plainly see that Nim was more than a bit unsettled.

She brushed her hands over the false skirt of her new constable wardrobe to straighten out a mess she may have felt more than seen. "Thank you for coming." She prayed he had not told Warrick, but it was no accident that she'd not requested Wes's visit until after the seneschal would have left to attend to his work.

Crossing to the table where she'd stashed her documents, Nim gestured Wes over. He stood opposite her, his concern evident.

She slid the documents regarding Lord Preston across to him. Wes glanced down, brows furrowing as he scanned the correspondence and Nim's report. There was no way out of the trap Rhen had laid for them. Lord Preston may have been put into position to take Warrick's place as heir, but he could only do so if Warrick was removed. Warrick was too valuable to Stewart and to the kingdom. But she needed to know what Wesley knew and that her friends would understand what was at stake, even if it was impossible for them to forgive her for what she meant to do.

Wes released an unsteady breath then pushed the documents back. "Don't pursue what you've dug up with Lord Preston, Nim. Please. There are things you don't understand. Things beyond any of us. I know he can't share everything with you, but you need to trust Warrick."

Margery had been right about Preston, then. And Wes did not want her to interfere in whatever the king or Warrick had planned for the man. Except Wes had one thing wrong: Nim did trust Warrick, which was why she knew without a doubt that he would risk everything to protect her. He'd proven he would do what it took without thought to her wishes. He had knocked her out with magic before and placed her in a wagon to be carted from the kingdom.

Rhen was coming for them, one way or another, and when Warrick tried to save her, it would destroy him and Inara. Stewart's heir could not be replaced by someone owned by the Trust. The queen would win. Warrick was all that held the kingdom's protection, the only thing that kept Inara from being devoured by magic.

But Nim was expendable. She had one chance to make things right, one chance to make a deal before Warrick could stop her. The kingdom had given up on her long ago, turned her out. The few who hadn't were her father and those like him, men and women who put Inara's safety above all else, who had sacrificed everything on a gamble, a child who might someday tip the balance. It was time to repay that debt.

Nim had heard of other kingdoms, far away, where magic ran

free and the suffering was endless and dark, unspeakable acts were carried out by those who had no restraints placed on their power outside of magic's own laws. She could not let that happen to Inara.

She straightened to face Wesley, hands suddenly steady, voice too calm. "I need you to deliver a message."

CHAPTER 20

Nim left the dagger on the mantel in her room. Warrick would find it—sooner than she might like, if the fates had anything to say about it—and know that she had gone through the secret passageway, an escape he had given her, to steal out of the castle while Wes and Maris had been distracted by her tasks. It was underhanded, she knew, but she could not take the time for regret when the Trust intended to take down Warrick and with him the future of the kingdom.

Dawn's light had chased long shadows across the square, and the morning sun warmed the block that lined the streets. Nim kept to the narrow walk at the storefronts, her pace swift and sure to a place she'd been countless times, a place to which she'd thought she would never have to return. The ring of hammer against anvil and the songs of the clothier echoed from shops on her way past. The streets smelled of baking bread and stinking dyes over lingering woodsmoke. To the people of Inara, it was like any other day. Turning down an alley, Nim tipped her head at passersby, only to be met with gazes that darted from her to anything else. It was not likely that she'd been recognized as an agent of the king, but she was near enough the gates to the Trust that no one wished to pay her mind.

Not thinking of them or looking at them were things that kept Inarans safe. They were living beside a den of monsters and knew all too well what waited inside. The long stretch of street before the gates to the undercity was empty of traffic. Trust business was conducted under the darkness of night, and even the last of the revelers would have cleared from the streets by the midmorning hours.

Two guards stood at the entrance, their trim jackets in accountant black. The gates were closed.

Nim swallowed hard, forcing down the instinct that told her to flee. She could not remember the last time she'd seen the iron gates down. Her boots were silent on the stones, coming to rest before the latticework of bars. "Nimona Weston," she said. Eyes forward, not allowing the sentries even an attempt to snare her, she waited. Neither replied.

"I am here upon invitation," she tried, biting down the oath that wanted to follow. The sentries did not flinch. Granted, most who knew Nim in the Trust tended toward loathing her, but she was not usually ignored. "I come unarmed." It wasn't entirely accurate or even applicable to her situation but worth a shot. She'd never considered they might not let her in—it had certainly been the least of her concerns. She sighed, resigned that she might have to give one of the guards her eyes before they paid her mind, and a laugh echoed from beyond the wall.

Rhen. She'd not even felt him. Fates, she didn't understand how he could hide from her so thoroughly.

Leaning against a stone column in the way he'd stood the first time she'd encountered him, Rhen rolled lazily from the shadows and into view, a finger tapping lightly against his chin. "Let her pass."

Neither sentry moved, but the gate jolted then raised before her. A realization rose with it that if she stepped through the arch, the gate would close again. Nim would be trapped inside. Her fingers trembled. Her feet itched to run. On the other side of the archway, Rhen's power swam. It did not reach for her, did not call or bind. He was letting her make the choice. Letting her, Nim thought, so that he would see what she might do. Not because he couldn't make her do as he bid. Not because he hadn't trapped her. Because he was curious.

None of it mattered. His gaze focused on her, and all she could see were the corners of his eyes, the curve of his lips, the way his dark hair twisted at his temple just like Warrick's. Nim had made her choice before she ever reached the Trust.

Striding forward, shoulders straight, Nim crossed through the gateway. She did not flinch when the iron bars slammed home behind her but only kept on as Rhen turned to keep pace beside her.

The main corridor was empty, a cold echo of the structure at night. Rhen led her not to one of the many sitting rooms and gathering halls that lined the corridor but to a moderately sized office lit brightly by trenches. When they crossed the space, he gestured to a chair then leaned his hips back against the desk before it, crossing his arms in wait. He meant to stare down at her.

Nim did not sit. "I've come to make a bargain."

His mouth twitched, but she felt no humor from him. He'd barely sent her an intimation at all. Perhaps the game was less fun when he'd already won. "Lady Weston," he said, "I cannot express how delighted I am."

"You do not seem delighted at all."

He smiled. "Yes. Well, I suppose I should not like to reveal my hand until I've heard precisely which bargain you've come to agree upon." He uncrossed his arms then curled his palms around the edge of the desk and leaned forward a fraction. "Forgive me if I am not entirely forthcoming with faith in a woman who recently stabbed me."

A shiver of fear ran over her skin. "As you say." She paused to swallow. "I was the one who acted against you. I am here to reconcile the debt." And to keep the Trust from taking their recompense from Warrick, hurting him, or outing him so that he would be hanged on the square. Nim gave Rhen a level stare. "I am the sole party responsible for the act. Only me."

His smile twisted into something that spoke of real pleasure, but he let Nim sense nothing more from him. She understood he might still act against Warrick, but it would not be because of her. It would not be made legal by her crime. Whatever Rhen did after she made her bargain would cost him, not Warrick. Rhen straightened, walking around the desk as he said, "Yes, I see that you mean to have it done before the Trust takes its own actions. Terms, then..."

He reached for quill and parchment, but Nim's voice drew him up short. "No."

Rhen glanced up from his desk, genuine confusion teasing at the edges of a more concealed emotion.

He could not be trusted—no one who dealt in magical contracts could. And if she were to make a bargain with any of them, it would be the youngest brother. Rhen might give her what Calum would not. He didn't care about the rules and gave no indication that he was in the game for anyone but himself. But Nim knew better. Bargains were for fools. She would only find herself further entangled with the magic, bound by tithes and unable to gain freedom ever again. She did not need a brief reprieve. She needed the game to end.

Nim stared into Rhen's dark eyes, her words a vow. "I will only bargain with your queen."

A startled huff came out of him. He placed a hand to his chest, gaping back at her, and apparently realized she was entirely serious. Then the laughing started, a full-on fit from deep within his chest, loud and genuine and not very gentlemanly at all, to be honest.

She let him get it out of his system. When he finally straightened, wiping at the corner of his eye as he looked back at her, his grin as wide as a serpent, she said, "Take me to her. We don't have much time."

"Indeed," Rhen said after a moment of shaking his head. "In.

Deed." He chuckled one last time then adjusted the hem of his jacket and held an arm forward. "Come, Lady Weston. Let us deliver you to that queen."

⁂

THEY WALKED through the undercity in eerie quiet. Everything felt sleepy, as if the magic slumbered and the revelers and Trust associates had fallen with it. Nim's steps were lighter than they might have been but not because she felt under its spell. She, it seemed, was afraid to wake it.

Rhen did not glance at her and did not utter a word but walked with muted purpose through the halls. The path wound deeper into the undercity, toward the well of power that had so often thrummed through Nim's veins, toward the magic she had tried so hard not to think of since she was a girl.

It was said that the head of the Trust could not leave the well of power. But just because a thing had not been done did not mean it could not be.

Nim had never seen the woman outside the undercity. Surely, she had left before, perhaps under the cover of night, perhaps long ago. She had met with Stewart—their son was proof of that. Unless, of course, she'd found a way to draw the king beneath the kingdom and to her lair. Nim might never know, and she wasn't certain she wanted to. But she understood that the power fed the head of the Trust's magic. She understood that if Calum or Rhen—or anyone who had no fear of leaving the undercity for the streets of Inara—inherited the magic, the kingdom would fall.

Perhaps there was truth to the rumor. Perhaps something did tie the queen there. But if it did, it was something Warrick had been able to walk away from and something Nim wanted no part of.

And yet, it was a part of her. She could feel it even now, like the purr of a sleeping cat, a mythical beast from childhood tales come to life, more real and terrifying than it had any right to be. It would wake and snare her, and Nim had no means to fight back. She was human. Inaran.

She was a fool to even try.

Over the years, Nim had done her best not to think of the queen by name, just like everyone else. Even if the superstitions of Inara were nonsense, she had learned the hard way that for her, some were true. Thinking of the head of the Trust and remembering what she had done to Nim's father... such things were more than dangerous. They could be used to draw her in.

Never mind that she was about to walk into it willingly.

Rhen held the door to the queen's chambers open, his posture that of a man aware of his station. "My lady," he said with a little dip of his head, inviting her to go before him.

Her heart seized for a beat, but her feet kept on. It was the same chamber from so long ago, with high, vaulted ceilings in the same dark stone as the main corridors, a smooth and even floor, and sparse furnishings. Throughout the space ran a system of trenches flickering with quiet, magic-bought flame and half a dozen dark springs resting like open pits across the floor.

"My queen," Rhen said from beside her, and Nim had the sense that she was the object of a private jest, that it was not what he usually called her. "We have a guest."

A figure shifted in the shadows, and Nim found herself entirely frozen despite her basest instincts screaming to run. The light in the chamber flared brighter as the figure moved closer, coming to the center of the floor with a practiced grace that fought with the upturn at the edge of her mouth for which seemed more deadly. Beneath a thin silver crown, her dark hair was bound in a set of uncomplicated braids to reveal a long, slender neck and bare shoulders. Her gown was simple and unadorned, its shape presenting nothing as much as the lean muscle and steady poise of the woman beneath. "Rhen," she said like the purr of that sleeping beast. "How lovely of you to bring us a gift."

Nim had never been particularly annoyed at being the target of such jabs, but that the Trust found so much pleasure in toying with her life seemed to burn right through her fear—or at least a fair portion of it. The head of the Trust was a tyrant and a murderer, and yet, she had the audacity to mock someone she'd ruined as a child.

"Your majesty," Nim said. "Mere days ago, I was stolen from the streets of Inara while about king's business, kidnapped by Trust accountants and dragged below to what I can only presume was my father's cell." She could not feel a single intimation from the head of the Trust, but beside her, Rhen's promised delight at her visit had blossomed into something tangible. Shoulders straight, Nim kept on. "He has since proceeded to trespass on kingdom property by invading my rooms, the castle gardens, a gathering, and a ball. While I cannot claim complete knowledge of the rules binding Trust associates, at least some portion of those events must be in violation of your laws, as they are certainly considered criminal offenses in Inara."

At her side, Rhen had a nearly physical reaction to her words. She wasn't certain if he meant to burst into laughter or cuff her on the back of the head.

The head of the Trust looked back at her, apparently unmoved, but the tip to the edge of her lips remained. She did not seem to dislike the affront Nim provided. Without speaking, the queen's dark eyes shifted to her son.

"She stabbed me." Rhen's tone was smooth, the words somewhere between defense and quip.

The head of the Trust blinked. Rhen shrugged. He did not seem to be even remotely interested in adding that the dagger had been woven with Warrick's magic, that his threat for recompense was the very reason Nim had come. Rhen tilted his head to give her a conspiratorial grin.

She realized she had turned to gape at him.

He bit his lip. "Well," he said, "I suppose I should leave you to your bargaining, Lady Weston." He gave a half bow. "Mother." Then he was gone.

Nim felt as if all the air had left the room. She wasn't sure she was breathing. She didn't know if she could remember how.

The head of the Trust stepped closer. Nim's gaze snapped to her, and suddenly, her breath, her heart—her fear—had risen from the ashes to burn again. She cursed.

"Lady Weston," the queen said, as if testing out the name and deciding it did not suit. She did not seem to have aged a day, and though Nim was not the little girl she had been during their first encounter, the head of the Trust seemed no nearer to Nim's size.

Nim felt as if she was being towered over, as if the woman made her somehow smaller. She stared at her, the single person who had stolen so much from her, a being that felt of pure power, an unstoppable force.

The queen's mouth shifted into a grin. Her incisors were sharp—a trait she'd given each of her sons, Warrick included. There was nothing warm or pleasant in her smile, though, and nothing teasing like Calum's or gamesome like Rhen's. The head of the Trust had no need to charm Nim, not when she had her on a tether to draw her near at will. There was no illusion of control—Nim was only alive because the queen was allowing it. Everything that had happened had led her to the queen's hand.

"Get out of my head," Nim said through gritted teeth. The queen's grin spread to her eyes. Hands curled into fists, Nim stood her ground with what little strength she had left. "I have your heir locked in a cell, bound by contract."

She shrugged. "I have another."

Nim's legs trembled so savagely she feared she might fall. If she did, she knew she would never get up. She would be crushed beneath the weight of the magic. Devoured. "What do you want?" She'd meant the words as an angry hiss, but they came out little more than a plea.

The queen took another step closer to stand directly in front of Nim then reached forward to tilt Nim's face toward her.

There was a moment of stillness in which Nim could only hear the beat of her own pulse, in time with the magic. It begged her to give in, to step from the edge of the precipice and fall to the darkness that waited below. The queen said, "Kill the king."

Nim's heart kicked hard once before resuming its pace. More games. "That's not what you want."

The queen's smile returned. She was too close, the magic too intense, while Nim wondered if it had been a test and what might have happened if she'd agreed. The head of the Trust did not need Nim to kill King Stewart. She could have done so at any time. She only wanted control of his heir—the rest, she had surely worked out already. The heir was her son, after all. But Nim was her key to... *something*. Nim had been her plan all along —otherwise, the bargain the queen had given to her father would never have been that Nim would chose the heir's fate.

The queen plucked her fingers from beneath Nim's chin. "'Get out of my head,' you say, as if you were not rooting through our thoughts like a rabbit in the gardens." She clucked her tongue. "Indecorous for a lady of your station."

The words were a slap. Nim wanted to scream and rage that she was no lady, that she had no station, that it was all because of *her*, that the queen had taken everything. But Nim's tongue could not be found, because somewhere in the back of her mind, beneath the terror and helpless rage, what she said had registered.

It was Nim's doing. Nim had gotten into their heads.

The queen straightened. "Well. You've done it now. The Trust must claim recompense for your injury to an heir." She shook her head. "Honestly, stabbing? Did you think to kill him with a mere blade, or were you aiming to steal his blood so that you might trap him in a binding as you've done to his brother?" Her words seemed to say, "How much trouble can you cause for my sons?"

Nim found her mouth agape. "You did this," she managed. "You have orchestrated the entire—"

Nim's words cut off as her throat was crushed, her feet dangling midair as she was suddenly jerked from the floor to hover at the queen's height. "Hold your tongue, Miss Weston, should you ever wish to use it again."

She had forgotten, lulled by the magic. The head of the Trust was not a woman, not a mere queen. A strangled gurgle was all Nim managed before she was unceremoniously let go from the chokehold to slam onto the stones below. Blood ran from her elbow, warm and thick, and her pulse slowed with the magic into a sleepy, muffled tick. Her head swam. Allister's tonics had helped, but they would not be enough. She needed to get her cursed plan done. Warrick had made a deal not to come to the Trust. Nim had to make her bargain before he realized where she was, or it would all be for naught.

"Put her in a cell," the queen said, turning away from Nim as if she were nothing. "Something dark and low."

More figures shifted from the shadows, and Nim's fear spiked anew. She hadn't realized they were not alone. She had not sensed the others at all. Unable even to push up to standing, she scrambled toward the queen. "No, wait. I come to bargain. I come to—" *To what—save Warrick?* She'd done no such thing. Rhen had not even mentioned him. For all Nim knew, the Trust had no idea he'd been stabbed with Warrick's blade.

The queen stopped before the shadows, not turning to look. Nim had the sense she'd not paused to listen to the entreaty, but she dared not waste the chance. "A bargain," she said. "Leave Warrick alone."

A thin huff of a laugh escaped the head of the Trust, one that said it wondered what the lady Weston thought she had to offer a queen.

"Just leave him be. Let him live. And I'll give you… whatever you want. Whatever you want with me."

She turned as a real laugh finally broke free. "Miss Weston, I already *have* you."

The door to the chamber slammed open, and splintering

wood erupted from the denotation to shower over the stone in a thousand brittle knives. Nim fell into herself, curling her arms over her head on the stone as the pulse within her exploded. *Awake.* The magic was awake. Worse—a thousand times worse—she felt what the queen had been keeping from her. She felt what had busted through the door.

Magic, warm and safe and absolutely deadly with rage, rose through her.

Nim glanced up in time to see a smile spread over the queen's face. "Warrick," she said. "*Son.* So good of you to come."

CHAPTER 21

Terror brought Nim from the floor, but she'd no more than pressed herself to sitting when Warrick was at her side. She stared up at him as his eyes bore into the queen's. An unspoken message passed between the two that was not an intimation but a *knowing*. The head of the Trust had played him, forced him into the move.

But it was not the Trust. It had been Nim. He finally broke the stare he'd trained on his mother, and the guards who'd come for Nim retreated toward the shadows. "Leave us," the queen said.

Nim did not hear the door close behind them, but she wouldn't have. Warrick had busted it to shreds. His gaze fell to hers, his chest rising and falling with an intensity that was rare, even if it did nothing to match her own. He loved her. He'd risked everything for her. But his intimation only said, *What have you done?*

Nim stared up at him. "I was making a bargain." She had tried to save him from the very trap he'd walked into. She didn't need intimations—her tone clearly said, *What have* you *done?*

His jaw went tight, his mouth a hard line. The fury of his

155

magic still raged as he knelt beside her, eyes flicking over her as if searching for visible wounds. The burn in her elbows reminded her that she had been hurt and that her blood was pooling on the floor. Warrick did not reach for her. Something about his response seemed as if he was afraid to touch her at all.

"Rhen said they were coming for you," Nim said, "to make you pay for what I had done." Her face was wet with tears that she had not realized she'd shed. She tried to will him to understand, to see that Inara would have paid the price and that she was the only forfeit that made sense.

"You don't understand." His voice was tired, the fury in him ebbing, formed into something cold but not resigned.

"Well, whose fault is that?" she snapped in barely more than a whisper. His answering intimation doused her momentary righteousness in ice water. Nim didn't understand what she'd done, what she had cost them both. It didn't matter that she hadn't known. It only mattered that it was done and could not be taken back.

"Will the two of you eventually stop this bickering, or is this how things generally carry on?" Rhen's voice was conversational behind them, the man having apparently come through the shattered door without a sound. He would have sensed the magic like her—or, rather, the way she might have if the queen had not misled her attentions. With Rhen's return, Nim wished, just a little bit, that she'd brought the magic-woven dagger and might have another go at the crime that had brought her there.

Warrick had not so much as flinched. He must have sensed his brother before he spoke. Between the magic and the loss of blood, Nim was feeling faint, diaphanous. "Warrick," she whispered, the sound a brush of air.

The head of the Trust rolled her eyes, though Nim wasn't certain exactly how she knew that, as her own had fallen closed. Then a spike of magic flashed through her and she was on her feet, dangling weightlessly between two of the queen's sons. Sucking in a hard breath, her head snapped toward Warrick.

His glare was on the queen. "Release her."

His mother's mouth twisted into something of a smile. "You know the cost." She made a sound of utter disappointment. "Honestly, Warrick. Using magic against your own blood?"

Warrick said a curse that Nim was fairly certain she'd never heard and was entirely convinced inappropriate to be aimed at one's mother, no matter how horrible she was. Nim was trying to process that the queen had feigned ignorance of Warrick's involvement until he stood before them while she fumbled for the pocket at her hip. She could not feel her fingers, and her thoughts were murky. A hand found hers, moving it out of the way, and she lurched—or attempted to—when she realized it was Rhen. His expression had lost its playfulness, and he only held up a vial for her to take. Nim looked back at the queen, who appeared baffled by the exchange, then Warrick, who seemed unable to touch Nim while the queen's magic was wrapped about her.

She's more fun when she's awake, Rhen said or thought. It was becoming very difficult to tell.

Nim downed the tonic, blinking hard as she lost her fingers again and the empty vial clattered to the floor.

The head of the Trust stepped closer, gazing at Warrick. "It seems you owe a debt."

"It will be paid."

Needles of pain teemed through Nim's fingers. Her elbow and shoulder ached with the burn of opened flesh, and her hip throbbed.

"She stabbed an heir," the queen said, "with your magic." Nim was fairly certain she'd missed a bit of the conversation, but focus was coming back, and for all that was sacred, it *hurt*. "The answer is not complicated," the queen told Warrick. "You know what I want. Remove that fool and take his throne."

"You know I cannot." The voice coming from Warrick was so angry, so raw, she nearly did not recognize it. Hopeless loathing swam beneath his anger, though it was difficult to tell whether it was for the queen or the bargains that bound him.

The head of the Trust stepped closer. "You have a choice, my son. Recompense may be paid by you or by her." Her dark eyes skimmed over Nim hanging slackly, bleeding onto the chamber floor. "Perhaps do not wait, should you have regard for her fate at all."

Nim thought she sensed something like a wince from Rhen, but she could not take her eyes from Warrick's face. They had brought him into the undercity, a place he'd been bound by contract to avoid, and that was not enough, they were going to make him choose. She would take the punishment for stabbing Rhen, or they would make Warrick take it for her. Nim had the feeling a punishment crafted for him would far outweigh her own.

"No," she said. "I've already told you"—her voice gave, and she swallowed hard—"I am solely at fault. This is my debt to pay."

"Calum goes free," Rhen said from beside her. "The terms are broken and your deal forfeit."

"What? No!" Nim felt ragged, bruised, and spent, as if a horse had dragged her through the streets of Inara on a very long rope. "I did not break our terms. I *own* him."

The queen huffed a disbelieving laugh.

Rhen cleared his throat. "Not your terms, my lady. I was speaking to Warrick."

She stared at him. Warrick had broken his contract when he'd set foot into the Trust. Calum was free to enter the kingdom at large—what else, she didn't know.

"Though," Rhen told Nim, "now that you've stabbed an heir, your contract is void as well." He gave her an apologetic smile. "I might have mentioned so earlier, but forgive me my fun." His gaze shifted to Warrick beyond her. "Besides, it's not as if our brother could not stand a bit of humbling."

Nim turned to Warrick, the blood draining from her face. He

looked down at her, his expression grave. "You knew," she said. He'd known Calum would be free, that what she had done to Rhen had broken the law and forfeited her hold over him. The king likely knew as well. It was probably why Warrick had been summoned, why he finally discovered she was meant to be hanged. Nim's knees went weak, but the magic held her firmly in place.

"They could not have retrieved him from his cell," Warrick said.

Not until Nim had escaped and run to the Trust instead of following his plan to keep her safe from the king, and not until Warrick had followed after her into the undercity. He'd broken his terms because of her.

And Nim had put Inara in peril to save him.

The head of the Trust made a disgusted sound. "Enough of this. Calum will go free. Nimona Weston's crime against the Trust requires recompense." Her tone was a warning. "*Choose.*"

Warrick straightened to face her. "I will not."

An angry huff of air escaped the queen, quite like an answer in itself. Then she flicked her wrist. "So be it."

Time seemed to slow, hanging stupidly like Nim's own mouth as she stared into the space before her. Distantly, she felt her hand raise to her stomach, felt the warm, wet spread of blood escaping between the fingers she'd pressed to what she realized was an open wound.

Nimona Weston's crime had been answered. Nimona Weston had just been stabbed.

Time returned with violent clarity, and she slammed to the cold stone floor beneath her.

✦

WARRICK SCREAMED. It was more of a roar, to be precise, but the magic that came with it tore through Nim as sharply as sound. The queen had stabbed her—not with an actual, physical blade, but she had rendered in Nim's own flesh the wound Nim had given Rhen. Her body was afire with pain, her palm pinned tightly against her stomach as Warrick pressed his hand over hers. He was touching her, and that was something, but she was fairly certain it would not be for long, not when her limbs were already going cold enough that they'd begun to shake with tremors.

She could not quite get her lips to form words, or she might have spoken as he stared down at her with horror in his face as he repeated her name. He had not believed his mother would do it, not when Nim still had a part to play. It was *his* fault, he seemed to think. *He* had done this to her. His intimations ran together, his emotions too fast to track. Secrets he'd been bound not to tell her rushed past her attentions, slipping just out of grasp as one thought replayed in his mind, over and over.

Nim was bleeding out on the Trust floor. She was going to die because of him.

Kneeling over her, hand still pressed to her wound, Warrick turned to face the queen. "Bind us."

A cold, slithering sensation ran over her skin. From Rhen, she felt something of surprise. From somewhere else, dread, though to be fair, the last one might have just been hers.

"How dare you?" the head of the Trust said, her tone deadly.

With her chest heaving with a wracking cough that made her mouth taste of blood, Nim could say nothing at all.

Something horrible rose from Warrick, emotion tangling darkly with power, and with it, another roar. *"Bind us now."* He was close, shielding her, grasping for any chance, willing the moment to hang on just a little longer. The queen looked back at him with disgust. Warrick's voice went the coldest Nim had ever heard it. "If you do not let me save her, I will crush all that you hold dear. That is my vow to you. Upon my blood. Upon my magic." *Every single thing. Destroyed. Gone from your grasp forever. And I do not care what it will cost.*

An image of the queen alone in the darkness fluttered

through Nim before the room began to feel fuzzy. She missed part of the conversation but snapped back when the queen's voice went hard. "Calum," she demanded.

"I gave you my word," Warrick growled.

"Calum first." The queen's voice seemed to tremble, though Nim was not sure that wasn't merely her own shaking. Her body seemed so far away.

Warrick snapped instructions at Rhen, and then his presence was gone. "You've made your deal," Warrick told the queen. "Now bind us. For if she dies, I will break every covenant you have ever laid upon me." His tone seemed to imply that killing a queen was on the list, but the idea got very little thought before Nim's body erupted into flames. It was not a true flame, she realized, because while it burned like fire, it did not stop. It carried on long after she would have been ash, long after there would have been nothing left. It carried on so long that she felt as if she might rather the flame had been real. It felt as though the sacrifice she had given for Alice had been nothing but the stroke of a feather, as if all the magic that had ever touched her the brush of a summer breeze.

It felt as if she might never feel again. Like there would be only flames.

"Nim," Warrick whispered. "Please."

She drew in a gasp that seared her lungs with the fire, drew it all from her skin into her chest then lower, into her wound.

For all that was sacred, her flesh was knitting together where the magic had torn her apart.

Like Rhen. Like Calum. Like someone who used magic.

"Bind us," Warrick had said. Nim's eyes shot open to find him hovering over her, his expression grim. She could not seem to find her body or anything but the fire beneath her hands.

They were alone. The queen was gone. No Rhen and no guards. The stone was cold again as Warrick collapsed beside her and pressed his forehead to her temple, whispering words she could not comprehend. "Bound," he'd said before. *Bound.* Nim was tied together with magic, the fount of power that was the Trust tingling over her awareness, lulling her into a false sense of safety even as it steamed like dark pools in the pits of the queen's chamber and even as some part of her still warned, *Run*.

But she was alive.

CHAPTER 22

Warrick helped Nim to her feet, but though she managed to hobble with assistance, she did not have the capacity to ask the questions churning through her mind. She needed to get outside, into Inara, and away from the effects of the magic. She needed to think, to focus. Warrick's power felt as if it was threaded through her, something darker and more like the Trust beneath. She did not entirely understand what the queen had done. She could not fathom what it had cost Warrick.

They stumbled through the corridors to a throng of onlookers, men and women of the Trust, whose gazes locked on the pair, and revelers from Inara, whose eyes went wide as their seneschal escorted the new constable from the undercity, the pair of them soaked in blood. When they finally came through the gateway, Nim nearly collapsed with relief at the feel of the sun. Warmth, a sense of safety, and feelings of *home* flooded through her.

But there was no safety. Nimona Weston was to be hanged by a king. She opened her mouth but was stopped short by Maris appearing at her side, sword at her hip, her usual maid's attire exchanged for a costume more fitting for a queen's protector.

Maris. That was how Warrick had known. She must have seen. She must have—

"Take her to my rooms." Warrick's tone was nothing but a command. "If the guard touches her, they will answer to my blade."

If someone tried to seize her for the king, he meant. She swallowed hard. Maris nodded and took Nim's less injured arm, but Warrick held her just a moment longer, as if he did not want to let her go. "I'll be right behind you," he promised. "There is something we need to take care of."

Warrick's eyes were shadowed by something that might have been exhaustion or pain, and his mouth was pressed into a line that spoke of resolve. His intimations had never been clearer. He was fetching the magistrate from where the king had her occupied. He intended to name Nim his wife before the king ordered her hanged. "It will be both of us," he said, "or neither."

It was not a true choice at all. Stewart was not going to allow being threatened that he must give up his heir or accept the continued danger posed by Nim. He'd already made his opinion on the matter entirely clear. He was going to see her hanged, whether Warrick approved or not.

Nim realized the watching crowds had not merely assembled inside the Trust. Citizens of Inara were observing the scene from a careful distance, figures shifting in shadowed doorways, peering from the cover of alleyways.

Warrick's secret had been revealed—his association with her, at least, if not with the Trust. Not that he had Trust blood, though. They never would have believed that, surely. They could not know that and let him live. She searched Warrick's face. He pressed a kiss to the corner of her mouth. "Go. I'll be right behind you."

Maris drew Nim away and into a waiting carriage then signaled the driver to make haste before the pair of them had even settled in. Through a crack in the shuttered window, Warrick's personal guards were visible, following on horseback.

A dozen men at most, as that was all Warrick knew he could trust. Nim was prevented from wondering what of the rest as she realized Maris was fussing with her clothes. "What are you doing?" Nim asked, her voice a bit less rusty than she might have expected.

Maris did not look up from her task. Nim was soaked in blood. So much of it, too much that she had somehow managed it and still lived.

"I'm fine," Nim said. It was hardly true, but she did not want to be fretted over. She just wanted to go home. If only she knew where that was.

Maris smacked her hand away then scowled at Nim's noise of complaint. "I moved it gently from my way the first three times. You'll not get another chance, my lady."

"Don't 'my lady' me. You told Warrick I escaped."

"Aye," she said, wincing at the sight of whatever rested beneath the hem of Nim's shirt. "And I'd do it again. My loyalty is to the seneschal." She frowned, murmuring, "It is my duty to protect you, after all."

Nim's stomach was raw and pink, threaded with scars not at all like those on her shoulder. She felt sick and glanced away. "You should never have let him come."

Maris sighed. "I had no choice. By the time I caught up to you, you'd already gone inside." Her tone made clear that Maris had not forgotten Nim's purposeful misdirection of her during the escape, the inane task she'd been sent on to make certain she could not prevent the very thing Nim had done.

Nim rubbed a hand over her face then flinched as the movement tugged the wound on her elbow.

"I'm going to douse you in a tub of lye."

It was hard to say whether Maris was jesting, but the idea of burning her skin off did not seem like the worst that could happen. Nim sighed, and Maris squeezed her hand in what was probably meant to be a comforting gesture. But Nim still felt strange, unsettled, and tangled with the lingering magic of the

Trust. She'd spent too long deep in the undercity. She wasn't certain whether she would recover. "As if it matters, when I'm on my way to be hanged," she muttered.

Maris might have argued, but the maid instead had gone rigid at some signal or sound that Nim had not noticed. Her hand was on her sword, her eyes on the window of the carriage.

Nim was unarmed. She'd nothing at all, save her bloodied clothes and pocketful of tonics.

Then she felt a familiar magic easing past her chafed senses to slither over her skin. Calum was coming. A bolt of panic surprised her, as she'd thought herself thoroughly spent, but she moved on instinct, leaning across the seat to peer from the window. The carriage was passing the square, nearly returned to Inara Castle. A flash of the conversation between Warrick and the queen came to her. "Calum," she'd said. "Calum first."

Nim cursed. It was an especially vile one that brought Maris's attention back to her.

"Calum," she explained. "He's free. Warrick gave Rhen instructions, some way to retrieve him from the cell." Nim hoped, truly, that Rhen had not harmed the guards, though she could not remember precisely what Warrick had said. Only that the eldest heir to the Trust had gone free because of her.

She cursed again and then was opening the carriage door without a thought. Maris grabbed her, but as Nim turned, a current of fire shot through their connection. Maris jerked back, Nim's own reaction slamming her busted elbow into the frame of the door. She came off balance. The door fell open. She pitched backward through the opening.

Nim hit the street with a puff of breath, gasping as Maris scrambled after her. There was shouting, the clatter of hoofbeats, and the sound of the carriage wheels shuttering to a halt.

But it was too late. Around her, like the call she'd felt as a girl, the magic swelled stronger. It drew her, as it always had, to the source.

It pulled her to the square, to Calum and Rhen.

The men walked casually across the space, Calum's jacket slightly worse for wear from his time imprisoned, but otherwise as if a pair of lords were engaged in revelry and not the murderous heirs of the Trust, enemies of the kingdom.

Maris had hold of Nim bodily, and she and one of Warrick's guards tried to pull Nim back as the rest took up formation around them. The air went suddenly still, the banners ceasing their snapping, the bustle of Inara muted to a faint background noise as if the kingdom had been buried beneath a blanket of snow. Then an icy stream of wind whipped over Nim, stealing the heat of the afternoon sun and drawing loose strands of her hair to lash at her face.

The wind fell. A dozen birds took flight from their perches. Maris drew her sword.

"Lady Weston," Calum said from his place partway across the square. He'd moved closer as she watched, but he was not near enough that the guard would take their swings. Rhen bit his lip in gleeful anticipation.

Despite the distance, Nim had the urge to step back. Maybe what she'd just been through had left her too raw, or maybe she was only on edge, but Calum felt strange. Different somehow. More dangerous.

"What restrictions did the broken contract discharge?" Her voice was low, but she knew Calum would hear. The entire square had gone silent, sleepy, and unaware.

Calum gave her one of his lazy smiles. "Don't you know, Nimona?" He made a gesture that encompassed the square, one it seemed felt the absence of his cane. "I am allowed to run feral on the streets of Inara. Indeed, in your very home." He leaned forward, letting his words sink in. "I owe you a debt, Lady Weston. Expect it to be paid."

The echo of the promise he'd made in his cell rolled through her, a physical thing. When he became free, he would come for her. He intended to make her pay.

Calum meant to kill her, and not quickly.

The breath seized in her chest, not from fear but by Calum's magic.

Rhen leaned toward his brother. "Do let me keep her. It would be terrific fun."

"I'm free," Nim said when her breath returned. The force of her proclamation surprised her, but she'd never felt the truth of it more. Whatever Calum did, whatever happened with the king, Nim was owned by no one. "Nothing will bind me again."

The pair of them stared back at her, something wicked and satisfied in their grins, something that teased she was so very wrong.

"I am free," she repeated, "and Warrick is coming." Fates, she hoped it was true. She would have given nearly anything for his presence in that moment.

"Oh, I suspect he'll be occupied for a bit," Rhen said. He gave her a playful wink and glanced over his shoulder, where Nim realized the shop patrons and millers-about had begun to part.

Beside her, Maris swore. "The king's guard."

Rhen chuckled. "Apologies. I suppose it would have gone better for Warrick if I'd not alerted the guard of our exit." He bumped Calum good-naturedly with an elbow.

Calum never took his eyes off of Nim. His look was a vow. It might not be that day, but he would find her again.

The pair walked on, the square resuming its bustling no more than a heartbeat before king's men burst into the square in pursuit of the heirs to the Trust. Warrick's guard did not bother pointing out the direction in which the two had gone. Nim let herself collapse into her maid's embrace to be conveyed back to the carriage.

❧

Nim was returned to Warrick's rooms under the cover of guard, secreted passages, and the distraction of the entire king's army on the hunt for Calum and Rhen. Maris had seen her to a warm tub, where Nim soaked and washed and pointedly did not examine her wounds. Her hair was brushed and sorted, and she was draped in a long gown that fit loosely at the waist but dipped low to bare her neck and shoulders. She sat in Warrick's plush chair, a wrap covering her arms and an untouched plate of food on a small table nearby.

Staring across the space, Nim watched the wide, handsome desk she'd been sent to riffle through at Calum's command what felt like ages before. All along, Calum had known her connection to his brother and that she would decide the fate of the heir to Inara.

Wesley came in with a fresh cup of tea. He lowered himself beside her, passing it over carefully, as if she might break.

Thanking him, she wrapped her hands around the cup. When she opened her mouth again, wanting to give an apology, she did break, her voice not letting her speak the words. Fates, she did not know what she had done and couldn't know what was to become of any of them beyond that she could not tell Wesley goodbye.

He squeezed her shoulder. "All will be well, Nim. Trust in Warrick, as I trust in you."

She drew a breath that felt like a sob then realized Wes's expression had changed. "What is it?" she managed.

He shook his head. "Nothing," he said. "You just seem... different."

She did. She knew she did. But she did not know what it meant.

Wes gave her a gentle smile. "It will be well," he said again. "And I will see you tomorrow."

Nim took his hand a bit too tightly before he left. "Thank you, Wesley. I adore you. You are the bravest of us all, the most loyal and true."

He blushed. "My lady, don't say such things when morning will see you restored to yourself and you'll have to face me again."

She chuckled. "I would never deny it, Wes. Not at all."

By the time Warrick came, she'd finished her tea. He was dressed in full regalia, the coronet of his station upon his head. He crossed to her without a single glance at the room.

Kneeling before her, arms sliding into the chair at her sides, he asked, "Are you well?"

A helpless laugh escaped her, and it, too, felt like a sob. Warrick came forward to hold her, pressing himself to her and burying his face against her gown. He was sorry, still, but he would not have changed a thing.

"What do you mean?"

He glanced up at her, seemingly caught off guard that she'd read his intimation. "I need you to be strong," he told her, "for just a little while longer."

"That... does not sound pleasant at all."

His mouth shifted into an imitation of a smile. "Would that I could offer you only what was pleasant and take away all the rest." He lifted her hand to press a soft kiss at the center of her palm. "Would that I could give you only pleasure and take away our pain." His lips trailed upward to press against the delicate skin over her pulse. "Would that you might only feel what my love could bestow and not what it might steal away."

"Warrick," she whispered.

His eyes met hers again, and he drew back. "We've something more to take care of," he reminded her. "And it still waits."

She swallowed hard.

"But first"—Warrick's fingers slid down the length of her gown, tracing her hem until he reached the bared flesh above her slippered feet. His hand wrapped gently around her ankle, warmth suffusing her as his thumb tracked over her skin. He kept his gaze on hers as his hand slid higher, blazing a slow trail of heat up her calf, brushing the sensitive skin near the back of her knee, then sliding to the top of her thigh. His other hand followed, delivering the sheathed dagger she'd left in her room.

"This," he said, strapping the weapon to her thigh, "belongs with you."

Nim's mouth went dry as Warrick's fingers slid over her thigh, slipping at a torturous pace back down, again brushing the base of her knee, down her leg, and outside once more to settle the material of her skirt. He stood to stare down at her, never having taken his eyes from hers, then held out his hand. "Come, love. We will have this done."

CHAPTER 23

"It will be both of us," he'd said, "or neither." Come what may, they would face it together. Warrick intended to solidify his threat by going through with the marriage. Whatever Stewart chose, Nim would be Warrick's wife. The ceremony would be binding.

They would not both be hanged. Surely, no matter what the king ordered, he would have to let his son live. But Nim did not like that Warrick's determination to stand against his father's wishes might fracture their trust even further. Never mind that Warrick might simply have given the king his way at the start, because Stewart was right—Nim was a danger to Inara. She'd proven it only that day.

Nim had half a mind to tell him to forget it, that they should spend what time they had left concocting a plan. But Warrick had evidently devised several without her, because he seemed entirely confident that she would not die come morning. There was something dark beneath his intimations, though, something insidious that he seemed unable to look at for long, something he refused to look at with her at his side.

"What did this cost you?" she wanted to ask. But she was

terrified he might turn to her, brush a thumb over her cheek, and answer, "Everything."

It was a fairly specific imagining, and she had no interest in examining why. Instead, she wondered what hidden plans he and his father had in place and how she might have destroyed Stewart's careful strategy. Maybe he'd meant to use Calum against the Trust or to claim Warrick publicly as his heir. He might mean to announce a truce, for all Nim knew. The only thing she was certain of was that Stewart did not want war, not when he would so thoroughly lose. In any case, he must have devised some way to bind the Trust so that when Warrick was revealed as heir, there would be no uprising by the citizens because of his connection to magic.

Warrick squeezed Nim's hand, drawing her from her ruminations.

They had not returned to the tower that overlooked the kingdom but instead stood before an altar inside a private room outfitted with little more than shelves upon shelves of ancient texts and tables stacked with scrolls. Narrow tapestries lined the space between shelves, and a few dozen tapers had been lit near the front of the room. Beyond them, a tall door opened, and a figure dressed in long black robes stepped through. Her dark hair was pinned tightly beneath a head veil, the sharp lines of her face striking.

"Lady Sybil," Warrick said.

The woman inclined her head. "Seneschal." She turned narrow eyes on Nim. "Lady Weston."

Nim dipped her head, but she owed no curtsy to a magistrate if she was about to become a seneschal's wife. She felt Warrick's hand slip over her back, drawing her closer to stand before the lady Sybil.

"Your witness?" Lady Sybil asked.

Maris slid from the shadows and into view, nearly causing Nim to jump from her skin. "I bear witness, upon my honor and by my blood, before crown and kingdom, beneath stone and sky."

Nim felt her brow pinch at the phrasing, but her attention was drawn to the magistrate.

"Nimona," Lady Sybil said, "daughter of the esteemed Lord Bancroft and Lady Elisabeth Weston..."

Nim lost a moment to the sound of her mother and father's names, names she'd banished from her thoughts so long ago, but Lady Sybil raised a bound volume before her, the vows inside that would tie Nim and Warrick by law. Hand trembling, she reached to lay a palm on the fine leather case, her mother's silver ring gleaming in the candlelight on her third finger. Lady Sybil placed a palm over Nim's hand.

A shock jolted through her, not like the one she'd felt with Maris, but worse because it was a warning.

Nim startled back, and Warrick caught her before she stumbled over her own fool feet. She stared at him, eyes wide, some part of her still urging her to run.

"I'm sorry," he said. "I didn't think."

He meant that he didn't know she might sense it. He hadn't warned Nim that the magistrate, an official of Inara just like he and Nim, was one of the Trust. She possessed magic.

He drew Nim to him. "I trust her," he vowed, speaking the words with purpose so that Nim might understand that they were true.

Her gaze searched his. All this time, they'd been scouring records, looking for agents of the Trust. Lord Preston, she'd thought. It was only him, one single citizen who'd had ties to magic. She was wrong. "Who else?" she whispered.

Warrick shook his head. "I'm sorry, love. I'll explain everything. I will. But not now. We don't have time."

She might have argued, asked what in the name of the fates could be more important than those with magic in positions of power inside Inara, but she could feel that his words were true.

Warrick wasn't merely eager—he was anxious. The vows

needed completing so that he could keep Nim safe. His grip on her tightened. "Please," he said, "trust me."

Trust in him, the way she'd not done when she'd run to the queen. The way she'd not done when he'd sent her to steal back her own contract. She nodded. "I will. I do trust you, Warrick."

Something settled in him, warm and steady, and he drew her close to stand before the magistrate, where they said their vows. They swore their honor to one another before crown and kingdom, between earth and sky, from this breath to the last, and then Warrick leaned in, his fingers tensing at the small of her back as kissed her, softly and sweetly and with a relief that was palpable.

They were married. *Finally*. Nim felt a bit dizzy with the enormity of it but could not help but smile at the direction of his thoughts. She had the feeling Warrick had been near dragging her to those vows by force if their ceremony had been interrupted one more time.

Warrick, her husband by law and by vow, held her close in his arms. "Finally," she whispered back to him, only half teasing.

He smiled down at her and opened his mouth to reply, but Warrick suddenly went still—entirely and utterly without movement.

Then came the bells.

Warrick's gaze snapped to Maris, but the maid was already moving with Nim's arm firmly in her grip. "I have her," Maris said.

"The south courtyard," Lady Sybil told him as if listening to some sound Nim could not hear, some warning over the bells. They were responding as if he'd given them orders and they had been prepared to act, as if they knew what in the name of the fates was happening.

Drawing his sword from his scabbard, Warrick rushed from the room without another word. Whatever emotional reaction he had to the signal he kept tied far too tightly within. But Nim had seen his momentary stillness. She'd seen the grim set of his face.

"What is it?" Her words met silence as Maris and Lady Sybil watched the door through which Warrick had gone.

Nim stared, too, wondering how she'd let him leave. They had been married, bound by law and vow. Warrick was meant to have revealed his secrets and let her see what he had not been able to before. Nothing had changed. She stood alone, confused as ever. Then she felt a sort of awareness outside her own, not unlike the brush of wind over her skin, despite that the air was still inside the room.

She spun a glare at the magistrate. "You," she hissed, remembering suddenly who the woman was and what magic made her capable of.

Lady Sybil did not seem in the least appalled at Nim's tone and was certainly not apologetic. Nim jerked her arm free of Maris's grip. "The two of you," she snapped, finger going up to point at the magistrate. Nim did not take the time to argue about either of them attempting to hold her there but only squeezed her eyes shut, forced her focus clear, and slammed her arms down in a bit of a fit as she broke whatever hold Lady Sybil had placed on her.

Maris shifted a hand to the hilt of her sword.

It was a fight Nim would lose, but she dropped anyway, kicking out toward the maid. Maris was too fast. Her legs shuffled back then stomped on either side of Nim's, pinning her to the ground. Nim twisted bodily, trying to spin free of the hold, but Maris had her caught and only let her struggle like a cat pinned by its tail. The magistrate stared down at the display impassively, holding her bound volume loosely to her midsection.

But Nim's hand had already slipped beneath the material of her gown in her writhing, and her grip was sure around the handle of her spare dagger. Maris's eyes narrowed.

Nim drew and struck. Despite the maid's quick movements, the blade drove it true. The dagger slammed home through

Maris's boot, eliciting from her a startled gasp. Nim was on her feet, already backing away, but all she sensed from Lady Sybil was quiet surprise. Whatever she'd done to hold Nim back before, she'd apparently no intention of fighting her further.

Without another look at the maid, Nim turned to run. She'd only aimed to stab the boot to the floor, not through Maris's foot, which meant that the moment she overcame her short-lived shock and was free of the dagger, Nim would be caught. She ran full steam through the corridors, taking routes she'd not taken since she was a girl. With any luck, she'd take a wrong turn, and Maris would follow the better path instead of catching her charge.

The bells had fallen silent, but the halls still echoed with their alarm. It had been so long since she'd been privy to the signals of the guard, but the pattern aside, any bell, any sort of warning, was no good. It meant the castle was under attack. It meant a threat to the king.

CHAPTER 24

Nim burst through a pack of armed guards and into the throne room. The corridors had been filled with scurrying staff and courtiers, the cacophony of their shouts and warnings making no sense at all until she saw what was happening with her own eyes, until she felt it.

Cold stillness settled over the edge of the room as every king's guard and courtier lined the wall, as far from the throne as possible. The king's chancellor was making a sign meant to ward off curses while his ewerer cried. Thin mist rose from the floor, writhing like phantom snakes from its stones—magic manifested in ways that even those without Nim's senses could not deny. At the center of the room, Warrick stood alone, the back of his black robe impeccable over wide, straight shoulders. He seemed frozen, unable to do anything but watch as Stewart sat upon the throne.

The king had gone ashen, with scarlet lesions scattering his flesh as if he'd been struck by a strange, sudden plague. He stared at Warrick, his son, the single person left of his family and paramount in his battle with the Trust, the heir to Inara.

Stay, Stewart's gaze seemed to warn. *Do not step closer.* But his warning was meant only for Warrick, not Nim or the crowd.

179

It was not a plague, nothing of the sort. Whatever held back the other onlookers did not hold Nim back. She took a slow step forward, her slippered foot touching stone that seemed to sing with power. The mist snaked around her feet, caressing her bare ankles in a way that made her curse herself for not having worn her usual attire. She would have given any of the fat jewels Maris had tried to drape at her wrist for a decent pair of boots. There was a shuffling of the onlookers, and Nim glanced back to find her maid shoving through the crowd to stare at the spectacle before her, sword drawn. She was wearing a pair of unmatched boots.

Her eyes met Nim's, all calculation gone. Maris saw it too—the magic, the king, the thing that would come to pass—and her quest to find Nim seemed to fall away. Nim swallowed hard before looking back to the scene. She approached Warrick slowly, the magic beneath her feet growing stronger, bolder, licking up her legs to snap and hiss where it met the magic woven through the dagger at her thigh. It cracked and stung where it struck, tingled over her arms, and whispered to her promises that Nim did not want it to keep.

Run from here, her thoughts said, *as fast as you can*. But her heart beat with the pulse of the magic, every thump drawing her *near, near, near*. She did not slow beside Warrick but only glanced up at him as his face turned toward hers. His expression was tortured, and rage simmered beneath his intimation, but he did not move. Nim could feel the dark, insidious thing she'd felt before, held just out of her reach—the darkness that had come when he'd made a bargain with the queen.

Her step faltered as she stared at him, her stomach suddenly weightless, as if the floor had become an abyss. Warrick had made a deal with the head of the Trust to save her, a deal with a queen who had asked both Nim and Warrick to kill the king.

He seemed to read the path of her thoughts in her expression, and she felt his shock of betrayal even before she'd registered her own doubt. Warrick saw her make the connection as he stood before his dying father, and it was a dagger to his heart. Her mouth opened on a denial, but Warrick turned away, his emotions closing off entirely as he stared at the king.

"I'm sorry," she whispered and felt his devastation sink deeper still.

Beyond Warrick, still lining the walls of the room, the courtiers looked on. What they thought was impossible to know, but before them was a tableau no one could deny. Nim, outcast from society for her father's ties to magic, had been restored to the king's service by a seneschal who'd only recently gone to fetch her, bloody and beaten, from the Trust. He stood, even now, surrounded by the writhing forms of magic. They'd no idea they would be meant to accept him as king.

She took a steadying breath and looked at Stewart. He seemed even paler, his cheeks gaunt in the way of Nim's father when the magic had hold of him, when it was too late to draw him back.

The king might not have wanted Warrick at his side, not when whatever illness he appeared to suffer might be burned away by the citizens of Inara to prevent its spread. But he would have had no objection to her being burned, not when he'd vowed to hang her for precisely what she'd done—she had destroyed them, the king and Inara, and maybe Warrick's chance to remain heir. It was not a plague, in any case. It was magic, dark and vile. It tasted of regret, sour and sulfurous, and called her to it as it had since she was a child. But the magic was not why Nim had come.

He was the king. The king *was* Inara. Whatever Stewart had done, it had been in service to their home, to keep Inara safe. He did not deserve this fate.

She knelt before the throne, her knee meeting the step at Stewart's feet. "Your majesty," she said with a low bow. "I am made of regret. All that I have is yours. Dispatch what is left of me to do your will."

When her gaze rose to meet his, she flinched at what she saw —forgiveness and resignation but none of what she deserved.

"She's won," Stewart rasped. "You were merely a weapon that she wielded better than I."

His long fingers curled around the edge of the chair, strained white against his ring. The head of the Trust had not taken him easily. She might have—the sacrifice was already made—but forcing him to bear the torment was only part of her game. His suffering was not for Stewart alone. It was for Warrick, too, watching silently behind her, the same as the head of the Trust had done when Nim lay bleeding on her chamber floor. She wanted Warrick to witness, to know what she was capable of. It was meant to hurt, the same as it had been with Nim's own mother.

"You will not have given up so easily." Nim reached forward to take his hand. "Tell me what you've planned, what I might do."

Stewart opened his mouth to reply, but the magic swam past Nim, causing slithering unease. A cough wracked Stewart, his hand crushing hers as he bent forward to steal a gasping breath. She placed her other hand over his, glancing around the room for a sign of the source.

They were there, somewhere. She could feel it. She did not see Calum or Rhen's faces among the watching crowd, but whatever Stewart had meant to say was stolen by one of the queen's sons. For a moment, Nim's eyes met Warrick's, and a fresh stab of pain overwhelmed her fears. She followed his gaze back to the king. His tunic was tinged pink, and a red stream ran from the corner of his mouth. He'd gone even whiter, the lesions blooming like roses on a bed of pale ash. Nim cursed, right there on the dais. A wild desire to jerk her hands free of his hold and run drove through her, but Stewart's words held her still.

"You're all here," Stewart announced to the watching crowd, "and you can certainly see what she has done."

For a terrifying heartbeat, Nim thought he meant her, but

the *she* Stewart spoke of was a woman he would not name, not the head of the Trust, not when it might invoke her. As if such a threat could have hurt him anymore.

He tightened his grip on Nim, shifting so that he might sit taller, so that his voice might carry. But the courtiers were as silent as the grave.

"Many of you have been in Inara's service long enough to understand. You have seen with your own eyes. You have lost—" His words cut off for another cough, but Nim knew well enough what he'd meant. She had lost her father, her mother, her very home. "Because of her treachery," he said, "I've been forced to take measures unbefitting a king. To secret away wives just as the lot of you have so happily prattled about to your associations outside this castle." An unsettled murmur passed through the shifting onlookers. Stewart waved his free hand.

Nim looked back at Warrick, who stared at the king, stone-faced. She could feel him, raw and harrowed, and could feel nothing of Calum or Rhen beyond. She had not imagined the sense of one of them or the feel of their magic. She worried that one was still present and that he might somehow do worse than what he had already done and reveal Warrick as a man who held magic.

Stewart hissed in pain. Nim's gaze went back to his, but the king's attention was on Warrick. "It should come as no surprise to you all that only one of my attempts succeeded."

A strange sensation shot through Nim, something like a chuckle, sending her hairs on end. But there was a gasp from the crowd at Stewart's declaration, entirely outside what brushed over Nim.

He did not wait. He was running out of time. His skin had gone dry and powdery beneath Nim's hand. "In all my years, I have managed a single heir. One son to carry on the Stewart reign."

Nim's flesh went cold, her gaze finding Warrick. *Save him*, she wanted to scream. *Bind him, cure him, whatever you did to me.* But she could not. Revealing Warrick's magic would see him killed. And she knew it would not work because all she felt from Warrick was hopeless rage. He could not save his father, could do nothing to stop what she'd done.

She, the head of the Trust. Not Calum, not his brothers, but the queen.

Panic welled inside Nim, hot and sharp at what the queen had done. The head of the Trust had killed the king of Inara. The Trust had won.

Stewart was still talking, but his grip went suddenly limp in Nim's hand. As she swung her gaze back to him, her unease at the magic rose anew. He'd gone thinner still, suddenly so, at odds with the man he'd been only moments before. The unsettling urge to back away nearly took her, but she held firm. It was all she could give him.

"And so," he said, pausing to draw an unsteady breath, "I have kept him among my closest advisors, so that I might have him near." Before the crowd's murmurs could rise and overpower his voice, Stewart spoke again, his eyes on his son. "My sole heir, successor to the throne, is your venerable seneschal Warrick, my son."

Warrick did stride forward then, threat of burning be damned. He was no more than to the steps of the dais when a laugh echoed through the hall.

CHAPTER 25

The laugh rang through the throne room like the alarms that had sounded for the king. Shocked gasps rose from the crowd before movement shifted the group at one edge of the hall. Courtiers shuffled hastily backward, clutching their hands to their costumes, making signs to ward off curses. The king's guard drew their swords.

A dark-haired figure sauntered forward without a second glance at the commotion he'd caused. Beside her, at the knees of a king, Nim felt the darkness rise in Warrick anew.

Rhen gave a devilish smile.

"Ahh," he crooned as he came to stop before them, well away from Warrick's reach. He dragged a palm over his chest, as if wounded, and his eyes met the king's. "To be so publicly cast aside." He shook his head. "But it does hurt, truly."

Nim could not know what the king was thinking, but she could feel past the rage in Warrick's intimation that it was the first Stewart had seen of the queen's youngest heir. She felt, too, something far darker. Nim did not take her eyes off of Rhen but watched as he looked on, relishing the exchange between Warrick and the king.

Stewart was no fool. He took in the lines of Rhen's face. He

185

saw the saunter, the dress, the persona of a man who was born to a queen. A man who was one of the Trust.

"Yes," Rhen murmured. "That's it. I can see that you're taking it all in. Warrick's brow, the cut of his jaw." Rhen snapped his teeth then gave the king a playful wink. "That charming smile."

A warning sound came from Warrick with a very clear intimation that Rhen should run.

He only shook his head. "No, brother, it's far too late for that."

Warrick stood, but before he could move from the dais, Stewart's hold went tight—one hand in Warrick's, the other in Nim's. Warrick turned to look down at him, the only family who had shown him anything resembling constancy. In Stewart's expression, Warrick saw nothing but his own betrayal.

Rhen chuckled. "Perfection, that's it. That look right there. You're remembering your second encounter with our mother, putting together pieces you'd long since buried with the past."

Cold dread swam through Nim, her gaze going from Rhen to Warrick then the king.

"I wanted to tell you," Warrick said to the king. "For all that is—" He shook his head, fury at Rhen and guilt for his treachery nearly stealing his breath. "I wasn't able." *She bound me to it.*

Memories slipped past Warrick's guard of a dark night in the queen's chambers and a boy so small as to not understand. Before she'd given him over to Stewart, the head of the Trust had tied Warrick up in magic, making him unable to reveal the secret that Stewart had fathered a second son.

Rhen was not only heir to the Trust. Rhen was Stewart's spare.

The king's reaction to the most horrific of all possible betrayals stole over his entire being, and Warrick lunged forward to plead forgiveness, to make his father understand. It was too late for anything. The worst was done. "Please," Warrick begged. "Please."

"Enough of this," Rhen snapped, gesturing to the crowd. "They see what he has done. They see that the king has borne not one son but two." Rhen's posture took on a self-satisfied air, his shoulders seeming to want to raise in victory at what he had won and his smug smile seeming to want to steal over his lips. "They see that not only does my blood run with magic, but so, too, does yours."

Warrick might have turned to growl at Rhen as his baser instinct demanded, but his first concern was the dying man before him, the man whose grip had slipped from Warrick's hand.

The onlookers had roared to life, though, the revelation apparently taken with more than a little doubt. Rhen was responsible for the magic, surely, that was surrounding their throne room, that had attempted to take their king. Rhen could not be trusted.

Warrick, they knew. Warrick was seneschal, nearly above reproach. Warrick had just been named son of the king.

"I swear to you," Warrick told the king, just as warmth spread through the room.

"Enough," Rhen said again, snapping a wrist in the air with dramatic zest.

"No!" Warrick shouted.

Nim turned to see blood blooming from Stewart's chest, just where Warrick held his hand forward in petition. Just as Warrick moved, the king's breath seized, his eyes went wide, and then, suddenly, right beneath his seneschal's hand, King Stewart slumped to his death.

Rhen had killed the king before Warrick had a chance to right what they had done, before he could make his father understand. There was a heartbeat of stillness, then Warrick launched from the dais. Nim had not had time to as much as move before he landed strides away, directly on Rhen. The tangle of their bodies slammed to the floor, sliding over stone as the room began to rumble around them.

No, Nim thought, *no, no, no*. But when her mouth came open, her words fell dead.

Warrick stood over his brother, fire pouring from his hands, magic crackling around him in a vortex of power that was entirely visible to every soul in the room.

Warrick's magic had been revealed.

The Trust had managed the only thing worse than the death of the king. They had outed his heir.

Beneath him, Rhen laughed.

THE DAGGER at Nim's thigh seemed to burn with power, with a desire to drive itself through Rhen's heart. Nim was standing, Stewart's hand limp in hers, and able to do naught to stop it.

Rhen had won. Stewart was dead. The truth had been unveiled.

Beyond them, the room stared on in horrified shock. Maris was already moving, taking up arms along with Warrick's other guards. But the king's men outnumbered Warrick's, and the courtiers and court officials were drawing weapons of their own.

"Burn him," rose a chorus. "See him hanged!"

Then, "His magic has killed the king."

Warrick stood among the men and women of Inara, alone in the center of a crowd but for his brother, a brother confirmed to be not just the queen's son, like Calum, but Warrick's full blood. Son of a king. Warrick's chest heaved in breaths that Nim could feel like knife blades. What the Trust had done was too much to bear. And now, above it all, his people thought his magic had killed the king, while he'd only been knelt at the man's feet, begging forgiveness.

Because of Rhen.

Maris moved, and Nim rushed forward, the handful of Warrick's guards coming to rest between him and the crowd. Nim broke through their circle, her palm itching for the blade, the blade begging to steal from Rhen his very blood. It wanted. It craved. The magic was demanding a sacrifice.

"Stop," Nim said. "Warrick, please."

He did not look at her but seemed to come awake to his surroundings, to finally take in what the crowd meant to do. They inched closer, their weapons not merely for show. They had learned one thing of magic, and that was that it must be stopped. It could not be allowed liberty in the kingdom, not if any of them ever meant to stay free themselves.

They may have raised Warrick from a child, but they meant to kill him.

The realization did not hurt Warrick. He did not seem to even mind. He had known, all along, that his secret could not be borne. What had his attention was the calculating glint in his brother's eye.

The Trust had driven them to this moment. The queen meant to take the kingdom, to free herself from the binds of the undercity and rise unchallenged, to devour the kingdom and steal from it sacrifices until there was nothing left and she ruled all beneath stone and below sky.

Nim felt a sickening twist in her gut at what Warrick was thinking—but no, because he was right. Calum and Rhen might have been heirs, but the head of the Trust meant to seize the throne and take all of Inara as her own.

Nim's head spun, Warrick's fury and the driving magic too much to bear.

"You have a choice," Rhen said from the floor. "Surrender to her or die at the hands of those who surround you."

An arrow loosed from somewhere among the guard, flying straight and true past Warrick's own men to lodge through his shoulder. It was close range, too close. Nim cried out as he flinched and fell to his knees, near to where Rhen leaned back on the floor, resting on an elbow with one hand to his broken jaw and the other pressed tightly to likely fractured ribs. She rushed to Warrick and was nearly hit with a bolt of her own. It caught her off-balance, and she was on the floor beside him when the first blades clashed—king's guard against the seneschal's own.

They meant to kill them all. Right there before Stewart, dead on his throne.

The queen and her sons had planned for it and had planted a man to take Stewart's place.

You have a choice, Warrick seemed to think of Rhen's words. *Let the Trust win...* His intimation flared with sensations Nim could not decipher as the room suddenly came alive with fighting, but then he seemed to reach his conclusion again. *Let the Trust win or become a monster myself.*

He rose from the floor like the rising of a flood, magic exploding out from him in a wave. Nim and his guard, all the king's men, courtiers and court officials—all but Rhen—were thrown from their feet with its force. Wind roared through the doorways as if called from outside, tearing tapestries to sail through the room. The clatter of metal against stone started up from a trembling into a cacophony as the weapons of those who'd been thrown to the floor began to shake and rise, to join in the maelstrom driven by Warrick's power. They crashed to the walls of the throne room, useless in a fight against powerful magic.

Nim felt weak, crushed by it, pressed to the floor. She could only watch in horror, her hands over her head to cover the screams of those around her.

The Trust had done this. The Trust had given Warrick a choice.

And he had taken it, taken it like the blade at her thigh that had screamed for blood.

Let them win, he had decided, or seize the throne himself.

CHAPTER 26

Warrick had painted the throne room in blood. Wounded guards and courtiers covered the space, not a single left standing. He stood at the center of the chaos, shoulders back and hands curled into fists. "Go," he told his brother. "Go to her and tell her what she has done. This blood is on *her* hands, and I will repay her in kind. She will suffer until she prays for her own end. Tell her," he said, "that is my vow."

His voice was raw, his intimation cold and deliberate. Rhen got to his feet, neither gracefully nor graciously, and gave Warrick one long look before he turned to go. His eyes skirted Nim's, though she felt that the lift of his brow was meant for her alone.

The dagger still wanted to stab him a bit.

She drew an unsteady breath, staring up at Warrick from the floor at his feet. Magic still crackled in the air around him, bright in his eyes, tugging at his cloak and hair. His jaw was hard. Nothing about what was coming with the Trust and Inara would be good. When Rhen disappeared from view, Warrick's gaze turned to hers. "You have a choice. Make it now."

No one yet knew she was his wife, he meant. Word of the

ceremony had not spread—the court had no inkling that Nim was any more than a constable whose father had ties to the Trust. She could leave. She could hide.

She did not have to remain at his side.

It cut like a blade, and Nim was not quick enough to keep the hurt from her face, despite that she meant to. And her hurt cut him too. Because Warrick did not want her to go. He was making her the offer to keep her safe, to give her a chance. But the idea of losing her was impossible to bear.

"The kingdom has turned against me," he said in apology. "In the eyes of Inara, I am the enemy." It did not matter that he was the true heir. It did not matter that he'd had no choice but to seize the crown by force to keep it from the Trust.

Nim took in the room of courtiers, men and women who lay prostrate on the floor, subjugated by magic, living out their worst fear. They had vowed to protect Stewart, to secure his reign, and —if need be—to give their lives in order to keep the kingdom safe. Warrick had brought them to their knees in one breath and had rendered them defenseless with little more.

She had been turned away by those people as a girl, cast out from good society when her father had made a sacrifice to save them all. Nim had longed to return since, to finally find the Inara of her home. But Inara had never been the ideal she had imagined. It had been teeming with secrets even then. The truth had been outed, the darkness had risen, and Stewart and her father were gone.

But she would not leave.

Pushing down the emotions that clawed inside her, Nim took hold of Warrick's hand and rose to her feet. Never mind that Inara had turned against him—Warrick was the only thing left to keep it safe.

Nim would stand beside him. She had nothing else. Something eased in him as she joined him, but it could not quite have been called relief, even as he clung to it as if it was a lifeline in the dark and deadly sea of power around them.

Maris watched from the floor with the guard, her gaze moving slowly from their clasped hands to Nim's face. It seemed a look full of questions, and as Nim stared back, she found she'd a question of her own.

If Warrick hadn't made a deal with the queen to kill Stewart, then what had he sacrificed to save Nim?

A NOTE FROM THE AUTHOR

The year before this series came into being, I was bitten by a tick (the least sexy of vampires) while checking the mail (the least sexy of backstories). After finally being diagnosed with the tick borne illness ehrlichiosis, I was cured (yay) and patiently worked toward a recovery that has—as of the time of writing this—never come (boo). While writing Seven Ways to Kill a King, I was continually plagued by immune system issues and eventually diagnosed with a sleep disorder. Reading became difficult due to brain fog, thinking issues, and exhaustion, so I took refuge in regency romance audiobooks—a *lot* of them. One might be able to see where it has influenced my work. (Shout out to Tessa Dare's Girl Meets Duke series and Lisa Kleypas's The Ravenels.)

The Between Ink and Shadows series came into being during a very difficult time, global pandemic aside, and though parts of the work were torturous above and beyond the usual writing struggles, I am grateful for having completed it. I hope you enjoy it. If you manage to at least stay awake for the reading of it, you'll have done better than me. Thanks for sticking around and I hope you'll love what's coming next. <3

ALSO BY MELISSA WRIGHT

- STANDALONE FANTASY -

Seven Ways to Kill a King

RIVENWILDE STANDALONES

Beyond the Filigree Wall

Within the Hollow Heart

Upon the Riven Throne

- SERIES -

BETWEEN INK AND SHADOWS

Between Ink and Shadows

Before Crown and Kingdom

Beneath Stone and Sacrifice

THE FREY SAGA

Frey

Pieces of Eight

Molly (a short story)

Rise of the Seven

Venom and Steel

Shadow and Stone

Feather and Bone

DESCENDANTS SERIES

Bound by Prophecy

Shifting Fate

Reign of Shadows

SHATTERED REALMS

King of Ash and Bone

Queen of Iron and Blood

- WITCHY PNR -

HAVENWOOD FALLS

Toil and Trouble

BAD MEDICINE

Blood & Brute & Ginger Root

Visit the author on the web at

www.melissa-wright.com